Song of Mercy

BOOKS BY BRENDA S. ANDERSON

THE POTTER'S HOUSE BOOKS (TWO)

Hands of Grace
Song of Mercy
Season of Hope (Coming December 2020)

THE MOSAIC COLLECTION

A Beautiful Mess
Pieces of Granite
(Re-release Coming October 2020)

THE POTTER'S HOUSE BOOKS

Long Way Home
Place Called Home
Home Another Way

WHERE THE HEART IS SERIES

Risking Love
Capturing Beauty
Planting Hope

COMING HOME SERIES

Pieces of Granite
Chain of Mercy
Memory Box Secrets
Hungry for Home
Coming Home – A Short Story

THE POTTER'S HOUSE BOOKS (TWO), BOOK 12

Song of Mercy

A NOVELLA

VivantPRESS

Minneapolis, Minnesota

Vivant Press
Song of Mercy
Copyright © 2020
Brenda S. Anderson

ISBN-13: 978-1-951664-02-2

Scripture quotations are from The ESV® Bible (The Holy Bible, English Standard Version®), copyright © 2001 by Crossway, a publishing ministry of Good News Publishers. Used by permission. All rights reserved.

This novel is a work of fiction. Names, characters, places, and incidents either are the product of the author's imagination or are used fictitiously. Any resemblance to actual events, locales, organizations, or persons living or dead is entirely coincidental and beyond the intent of either the author or the publisher.

Cover Design by Marion Ueckermann
Front Cover Photo from Deposit Photos
Back Cover Photos from iStock Photo

Printed in the United States of America

20 21 22 23 24 25 26   7 6 5 4 3 2 1

Note from the Author

The 24 books that form **The Potter's House Books Series (Two)** are linked by the theme of Hope, Redemption, and Second Chances. They are all stand-alone books and can be read in any order. Books will become progressively available from January 7, 2020.

Book 1: *The Hope We Share* by Juliette Duncan

Book 2: *Beyond the Deep* by Kristen M. Fraser

Book 3: *Honor's Reward* by Mary Manners

Book 4: *Hands of Grace* by Brenda S. Anderson

Book 5: *Always You* by Jennifer Rodewald

Book 6: *Her Cowboy Forever* by Dora Hiers

Book 7: *Changed Somehow* by Chloe Flanagan

Book 8: *Sweet Scent of Forgiveness* by Delia Latham

Book 9: *When Love Abounds* by Juliette Duncan

Book 10: *More Than This* by Kristen M. Fraser

Book 11: *Faith's Favor* by Mary Manners

Book 12: *Song of Mercy* by Brenda S. Anderson

Coming soon!

Book 13: *In Spite of Ourselves* by Jennifer Rodewald

Book 14: *Her Christmas Cowboy* by Dora Hiers

Book 15: *Where Do They All Belong?* by Chloe Flanagan

Book 16: *Radiant Rays of Grace* by Delia Latham

Books 17 – 24: Coming soon!

Visit **www.PottersHouseBooks.com** for updates on the latest releases.

To music makers everywhere ~

Keep singing the song God gave you!

""Let nothing be said about anyone

unless it passes through the three sieves:

Is it true?

Is it kind?

Is it necessary?"

—Amy Carmichael—

Chapter One

Be bold, Stephenie Winter said to herself for the umpteenth time this afternoon. Daniel and Rita were counting on her.

Guitar slung in front of her, she stood by the microphone and took in a slow breath to calm the shivers, even on this warm, but rainy, May day. Then she began strumming the song she'd composed just for their marriage. Her gift to her brother and his new wife.

She hadn't expected them to add the song to their wedding program at the last minute, or she wouldn't have presented the gift at the groom's dinner last night. That had been stressful enough.

But she could get through this. She was bold.

She closed her eyes, pictured only the happy couple beneath the backyard tent, ignored the four rows of guests in front of her, and strummed with her perspiring hand. Then she added her shaky voice to the song.

The light rain pattering against the tent added a beautiful percussion to the music. Her voice came out frog-filled and timid at first, but once she got into the song, her nerves calmed, and her voice cleared, became confident. It always did, so why did she have near panic attacks whenever singing or speaking in front of others?

The song came to an end and, thankfully, the guests remained silent, their focus on the happy couple about to say, "I do." Finally, she could relax and enjoy the wedding.

She set her guitar in its stand and rejoined the family row with her two older sisters, their husbands, and two daughters apiece. Immediately, her youngest niece, all pinked up from her hairbow to her sandals, left her daddy's lap to cuddle on Steph's. This pure love was the best part of being an auntie.

And the best part of a wedding was always the reception, as long as she could avoid Uncle Henry and his dogged determination to see her married as well. He didn't understand that women didn't need a man to be happy. If the right guy came along, fine, but she certainly wasn't searching.

Daniel and Rita exchanged rings, and Steph could see her brother's hands shake—the hands that steadied a gun in his livelihood.

The pastor then closed his Bible and grinned at the couple. "I now pronounce you husband and wife. Daniel, you may kiss your bride." The small group of onlookers cheered as the couple shared a kiss safe for the children to witness. Rita added a kiss on her husband's cheek which left a red-lips tattoo.

"How long before he notices?" Carrie leaned over and

tapped the stopwatch on her Fitbit. "I'm guessing ten minutes. Winner gets to choose where we have lunch next week."

"Deal." Ginny, the middle sister, checked her old-fashioned watch. "Fifteen at least."

"Nope." Both her older sisters were wrong. "He won't realize the lipstick's there until after the first dance." She'd do whatever she could to keep him away from the bathroom until then.

As the sisters debated, and the toddlers squirmed, the just-weds stepped forward to hug and thank the guests, row by row. First, they exchanged hugs with Rita's mom, who sat in a wheelchair. Then they hugged Steph's parents. Even her dad had tears in his eyes.

She handed her niece to her sister and stood. Her sisters and their families followed suit. In the aisle seat, Steph was the first to congratulate the couple. Her younger brother braced strong hands on her shoulders, looked down at her, then at their sisters, with a glare that, no doubt, made criminals cringe and confess. "What are you three conspiring?"

"Us?" Steph splayed a hand over her heart, her jaw dropped in mock disbelief. "Conspiring?"

"We're just thrilled you found your match with Rita," Carrie, the oldest sibling, said over Steph's shoulder.

Rita chuckled and pressed her lips to Daniel's other cheek, recording another impression. She winked at Steph, letting them know she was in on their game.

"Why don't I believe you three? And why do I get the

feeling that my wife is involved?" He gave his bride a quick kiss. "Wife. I like the sound of that." Then he scowled at his sisters. "You've all teamed up against me somehow, haven't you?"

They all giggled in response. Maybe their contest should be who could guess how many lip tattoos would cover his cheeks by mealtime. Their little brother might be a fantastic detective, but he was so smitten with his bride, when it came to the lip imprints Rita loved leaving on his cheek, he was clueless. Steph had seen him walk around for hours, oblivious to the mark on his cheek. Far be it from his sisters or brothers-in-law to inform him. So now, guessing how long it would take him to notice had become a frequent contest between his sisters.

With only thirteen months between Steph and Daniel, she knew him best and usually won.

He moved aside so Rita and Steph could hug.

"Thank you again for that beautiful song," Rita said during the embrace, then she stepped back. "I know that wasn't easy for you, but you rocked it. I couldn't tell at all that you were nervous."

Panic stricken, was more like it. "I'm glad I made it through."

Once hugged, she hurried down the white runner covering the grassy lawn and spotted Uncle Henry. Oh, she loved the man, but his favorite topic was her singleness. No doubt, he'd inquire why she hadn't brought a plus-one today and then urge her to find a man. His boomer generation failed to understand that women didn't need a man or children to be fulfilled.

She was Sassi—single and standing strong and independent—as were so many other women today. They just needed an ally to encourage them to be bold in their singleness without denigrating men. That was exactly why her vlog, *Be Bold & Sassi*, had become a hit.

Mom was already inside the house preparing for the meal, so Steph hurried to find her. Always the penny-pincher, Mom had offered to cater. In the process, she also volunteered Steph since she was "Sassi" and without children. Not that she minded helping, but being *told* to help was another finger jabbing in her direction, accusing her of being single with no kids, as if that was a bad thing for a woman in her mid-thirties.

With the success of her vlog, someday being Sassi would no longer carry a stigma.

She followed the enticing scent of tasty concoctions to the galley kitchen in Rita's house. Make that Rita and *Daniel's* place now. Yesterday, Mom had baked buns much of the day, and the aroma still lingered, making her mouth water. The roast had been cooking for hours, so it now fell apart in strings.

"Have you tried it?" Steph forked a piece of meat and brought it to her mouth.

Mom gave her a dirty look then laughed. "Of course. We can't serve guests something that tastes bad, can we?"

"No, we can't." Steph sampled the meat and it melted in her mouth faster than chocolate. Speaking of which... "Have you tried the hot cocoa?" Mom had her own secret recipe the newlyweds had insisted be served.

"You doubt it's good?"

"No, but I still have to sample it." She poured cocoa into the insulated mug that read "Steph" on one side, and on the other it said "Rita & Daniel" with the date. Each guest would receive their own mug as a Thank You memento for attending today. She tasted the cocoa and moaned. Yep, it was Mom's recipe to perfection.

"Now that you're done sampling, would you mind bringing the food outside? Your father recruited Dale and Terry to set up the tables." Her brothers-in-law could always be trusted to pitch in. Problem was, there weren't enough Dales and Terrys and Daniels in the world to go around.

She picked up the basket of red tablecloths and carried them outside. No surprise, mingling had already begun, so she'd better hustle with getting set up. She flung a tablecloth across the table and other hands gripped it, pulling it taut. Startled, she looked over at Uncle Henry.

Oh, snap.

"Looked like you could use a hand."

They sure could use help, but Steph had no desire to work side by side with her uncle. "All the food is in the kitchen. Mom would love some help carrying it out."

"Sure thing." He aimed for the house, but stopped and looked back.

Here it comes, the why-aren't-you-married-yet speech.

"By the way, I'm watching your vlog. Good job." He turned and headed into the house without a single spinster comment, leaving her speechless.

Had he just complimented her on her Sassi vlog? She rubbed her ears, making sure they were unclogged. Huh. Maybe he was finally getting it. Maybe this reception wasn't going to be so stress-filled after all, and she could enjoy it.

She finished dressing the tables while Uncle Henry helped his sister carry out the food. It wasn't a complicated menu, just pulled beef sandwiches, salad, and cheesy hash brown potatoes. About ten different kinds of bars would be served instead of cake. Mom had been baking since February when Daniel and Rita announced their engagement.

Once the tables were covered, she headed inside to see what else needed to be done. She carried out plates, silverware, and napkins, then set out the mugs on the coffee/cocoa table, dressing it up as artistically as possible.

"Everything looks wonderful."

Steph looked up into her little brother's eyes and she coughed to cover a chuckle. Four lip impressions now decorated her brother's cheeks. "Thanks." She came around the table and gave him a hug. "You look pretty wonderful yourself."

He tugged at his tie. "What we guys do for our women."

"We love to make you suffer, and I need proof of your suffering." To post on social media so all his work buddies could give him grief. She pulled her phone from her skirt pocket, planning to take a selfie, but then that would give away Rita's kisses. Instead, she waved over Howard, Daniel's mentor and best man, to take the pic, which he did while chuckling. She loved that everyone was in on the joke.

Howard handed back the phone and Daniel continued mingling. She brought up the picture and laughed. She looked amazing, and Daniel? Well, he looked good too. The poor guy. Growing up with three older sisters, he'd taken a lot of grief from them. But she always told him the ribbing helped make him a good cop.

She pocketed the phone then checked with her mom in the kitchen. "Anything else need to be done?"

Mom nodded toward the fridge, her hands filled with a tray of bars. "Grab a couple of water pitchers, then we should be good."

"On it." Steph took the water from the fridge and headed outside. Dad had the microphone clutched in his hand as he looked back at her and Mom. He nodded, letting them know he had this. Well, this should be interesting. Like her, Dad hated public speaking. She set the water on the buffet table then took a seat beside her mother.

Dad cleared his throat then congratulated the couple and welcomed Rita into the family. He was happy to see her add color to the Winter name.

Speaking of color, Steph glanced at Daniel's cheeks. At least five lip imprints were there, boldly. Rita must be freshening her lipstick between kisses. Oh, she fit right in with the Winter sisters!

Dad introduced the best man and the maid of honor, then finally directed everyone to the buffet table as music played from outdoor speakers. Well done, Dad! No one would ever know he'd hated every second of that speech giving.

All too quickly, the food was eaten, and the guys began pulling back the tables to create an intimate dance floor. The bride and groom separated, Rita going to talk with her maid of honor, and Daniel...

Uh-oh, he aimed for the house, probably detouring to the bathroom. If he looked in the mirror now, she'd lose the contest. She hurried to head him off, but Howard beat her, and then the men were talking in serious whispers. Probably something cop related—neither were good at leaving their work at the office. She walked in their direction and caught Howard's hushed voice.

"Yeah. If people would learn to speak up, stuff like this wouldn't happen."

Daniel's gaze shot her way.

"You're right about speaking up." She wagged her finger at both men. "It's your wedding day. There will be no cop shop talk, got it?" She mock glared at them.

Howard shrugged and Daniel raised his hands, surrendering. "You're right."

"Of course, I am." She turned to walk away then looked back and thumbed toward the dance floor. "Go find your bride. I think it's time for the bouquet and garter toss."

Daniel grinned. "Well, I can't miss that, can I?"

"Nope." And she'd just preserved her contest win. All she had to do was wait for after the first dance, and dinner choice would be hers. But in the meantime, she planned to get lost. No way did she intend to be around for the bouquet toss because she was the only single female adult present. Her catching the bouquet might encourage Uncle Henry and every other family member to tease her endlessly.

As Rita's maid of honor invited all single ladies—in other words, *her*—to the dance floor, Steph grabbed empty dishes from the buffet table and turned toward the house.

Those dishes were ripped from her hands. She gasped and looked to her left.

"*All* single ladies." Daniel nudged her toward the dance floor.

"But—"

"Get out there."

"You're gonna pay for this, Daniel Winter," she said under her breath.

He grinned. "Worth it."

Grumbling, she aimed for the dance floor, then took a sharp turn, angling away from the party and the house. She'd show them.

"Hey, Stephenie," Ginny shouted. "Heads up."

She looked back just in time to see the bouquet flying toward her face. She covered her face with her hands, and the satin bow caught on her thumb. No, no, noooo.

Cheers went up as she held the flowers loosely.

"When's the wedding?" one brother-in-law called out.

"Who's the lucky guy?" This from Daniel, the jerk.

"'Bout time you get yourself hitched!" Uncle Henry just couldn't keep quiet.

If they hadn't been in a family setting, she just might have told the guys where they could go. But she was an adult. She could be gracious about this. And she could make lemon cheesecake out of lemons. Holding her head high, she walked to the dance floor, knelt down as far as she could in her skirt, and called her nieces forward.

All four of the little cherubs ran toward her. From the bouquet she gave each a thornless rose. Then spoke to them, loud enough so all could hear. "This is a reminder to each of you to be Sassi like your auntie. You don't need to have a boyfriend to be happy, got it? Just be who God made you to be." Though she'd forsaken her family's beliefs long ago, she threw in that tidbit to appease them. "That's the most important *you* there is. Now give your auntie a hug."

Proud of herself, she stood and received hugs and "way-to-go" affirmations from her sisters. But not from Daniel, naturally. She looked around to find him. She spotted Rita, but no Daniel. Uh-oh, he hadn't.

She glanced toward the house just as Daniel came around the side, his cheeks now clean.

Shoot.

"I win!" Ginny called out.

Fine. Steph may have lost her mini battles today, but they'd both be fodder for her vlog next week. The men in her family had just waged war.

That closing song about choosing joy really spoke to Kyle Stevens. Pondering the words, he took his time packing away his guitar. This was the worst part about the move to a new church. It broke his heart whenever he looked out at the congregation knowing precious Evie wasn't there.

He couldn't blame anyone but himself, and that made it hurt worse. What was the matter with churches nowadays?

Choose joy.

The lyrics seemed to hound him. Convict him again.

"God made this day, and I will rejoice." The words echoed back at him in the empty sanctuary. Repeating, "I will rejoice' in his head, he picked up the guitar case and headed off the chancel area. Chancel. A word he'd only recently learned. At his last church, he'd played on a stage and more often than not, worshipping felt more like a concert. That was on him.

Nope. No more going there. Dad had told him often enough that mentally beating himself up wasn't healthy for anyone. Learn and move forward. If he wanted to teach Evie that lesson, he'd better learn it himself.

Still, even with the word "joy" nagging him, all he wanted to do was go home and have a pity party. Ending this chapter in his life hurt like the dickens. At least with moving today, he'd have little time to feel sorry for himself. Besides, Dad would kick his butt if he continued to wallow.

God would probably kick his butt too. He'd been doing that a lot these past couple of years. Why had it taken Kyle so long to notice?

He headed down the central aisle between pews. In front of him, the doors opened into the lobby.

Pastor Mitch Donner passed the doorway, then backed up. "Hey, great job today."

Words Kyle had once loved hearing, and had always

responded with the pat, "It's all God." *Hypocrite*. Now he didn't know how to respond without it sounding like false humility, so he just nodded to the pastor.

"Hey." Pastor Mitch laid a hand on Kyle's shoulder. "It's okay to accept a compliment."

Kyle sighed. "I know, I'm afraid of getting caught up in the accolades again."

"Don't worry about that." Pastor laughed. "We won't let that happen."

We, being the church, the people. Family.

"You're right. And thank you." Kyle managed a smile for the man who'd been his counselor and was becoming a friend.

"You sure you don't need help moving?" Pastor Mitch walked with him to the coatrack. Even though it was May, the temperatures assumed it was March. "I've got the day off."

"Thank you, but Dad and I can handle it. I don't have much." Ronnie had taken the most important thing—their daughter—so the rest of their "stuff" didn't matter. "But thanks for the offer."

After putting on his jacket, he led the way outside and waited as Pastor Mitch locked the doors.

"Well, if you change your mind, you know how to reach me." The pastor gave Kyle's back a light slap and headed for his sedan.

Now that guy was a good man, a true shepherd. One who didn't sugarcoat things or let bad behaviors pass because they were the norm outside the church.

And, as Kyle had learned, inside some churches as well.

He packed his guitar in the backseat of his Subaru crossover, then sat behind the wheel and prayed that God would remove the heaviness, that He would bless this day, bless Kyle's new beginning. Usually he left the service feeling upbeat, but today, in closing the book on his former life, he was missing his daughter big time. Making the move from the northern suburbs of Minneapolis to the southern suburbs felt a world apart from her, though she was barely forty-five minutes away.

Choose joy.

Only forty-five minutes. He could easily make that drive in an evening and get his Evie fix. Ronnie and her fiancé had promised him he was welcome to visit anytime. *Visit.* Oh, how he hated that word when speaking of his daughter.

He plugged his phone into the car jack, chose the "Joy" playlist, and headed for his new home: one side of a twin home his parents had purchased a few years back as a way to make money in their retirement.

They hadn't planned on his mom dying shortly after they'd moved. They hadn't planned on their then-estranged son moving in as a renter, either, so Kyle coming home was a blessing to both him and Dad.

Blessing.

That was a word he could grasp onto. See, choosing joy was already working.

Fifteen minutes of praise-filled driving later, he pulled into the driveway of his new home, his attitude reset. That was becoming easier as time went on. And to think that peace came as he arrived at the home owned by his father. Two years ago, that wouldn't have been a thought. Praise God for removing the veil from his eyes and heart.

He climbed out of his crossover, which he'd parked beside his father's pickup. The pickup should be all they'd need to get his final belongings. When his relationship with Ronnie broke down, and she walked out pregnant, he'd begun to realize that things carried little value. He'd let her have most everything they'd purchased together. All he'd required was equal time with their child when born, and thankfully Ronnie hadn't argued about that. If he had a bed to sleep in and his guitar, he'd have all he needed. Technically, he didn't even need those.

He carried his guitar into his side of the townhome and set it on the card table in the living/dining room. The home wasn't large, but had two bedrooms so Evie would have her own space. Yesterday, Dad had helped Kyle paint the nursery green, Evie's favorite color, although that could easily change two weeks from now when it was his turn to have her.

Adults really knew how to mess up kids' lives.

A knock sounded on his front door, tearing Kyle from his musing. Dad let himself in, something Kyle would have to talk with him about, just not today.

"Ready to go?" Dad looked around the living room which was sparsely furnished with the card table, a couple of folding chairs, and a couch and recliner Kyle had picked up at the local secondhand store. "Your place needs some life."

"Tell me about it." Ronnie would scoff at the lack of

design. Well, now that she was going to marry a neurologist, she'd be able to afford whatever design she desired. Kyle patted his pockets, making sure he had his phone and wallet. He gestured to the stack of copy paper boxes he'd scrounged up from around town. "Ready to head out."

No more words were shared as they grabbed boxes in each arm and made a few treks out to the pickup. When done, he sat in the passenger seat of his dad's truck, a massive vehicle Dad had used on his hunting trips. When he was younger, Kyle had often wished he'd liked hunting, but he couldn't get beyond seeing Bambi. Maybe if he'd liked hunting, they would have had something to talk about. Then and now.

"How was your music this morning?"

Dad was asking about the music? Kyle glanced to the left at his dad tapping out an unheard message on the steering wheel. "Uh, it went well." Kyle looked straight ahead, watching the rows of identical twin homes whiz past. What was the honest answer? That was what Pastor Mitch would ask. Don't reply with what the questioner expects or wants to hear.

"I'm getting used to the different style of worship music, but I'm liking it." Many of his former colleagues would call it old-fashioned, but he was learning there was value in traditional music as well as modern-day worship. Both had their place. "I really like that I can hear the congregation sing. It takes the spotlight off me."

"Always a good thing." Dad nodded and turned onto the

freeway ramp heading north toward Minneapolis. "Would you mind if I checked out your church sometime?"

Kyle's head jerked toward his dad so quickly, he swore he gave himself whiplash. "You like your church."

"Never said I didn't, but wouldn't hurt me to come hear you sing once in a while. You have a talent."

Another olive branch from his dad? He'd held out several during the past months, but this was the first acknowledgement of Kyle's gifts and chosen career. "I'd like that."

"Good." His dad's fingers continued to play on the steering wheel. A song maybe?

"Do you have a favorite hymn? If you let me know a few weeks in advance of you visiting, I can see about adding it to the worship set."

"They don't get any better than 'Amazing Grace.'"

"No. No they don't." He'd sung the hymn at his mom's funeral last year, and over the last months, the song had become his own anthem.

He couldn't help himself and started humming the tune, the lyrics running through his mind:

> *Amazing Grace, how sweet the sound*
> *that saved a wretch like me.*
> *I once was lost, but now am found.*
> *T'was blind but now I see.*

The words had been penned over two hundred years ago, yet remained true today. John Newton had been a wise man.

Beside him, Dad hummed along in his slightly offkey bass. "Will you sing it for me?"

Kyle held in his surprise over the request and began singing the first verse, his eyes closed, absorbing the words, turning them into a prayer. He moved onto the second verse, and the third.

And then silence took over.

Not the awkward quiet that used to hover between father and son, but the powerful stillness of two people bonding in worship. Goosebumps broke out on his arms, and Kyle prayed silently for his father, Ronnie, Evie, and once again asked forgiveness for the litany of mistakes he'd made over the years. And again, he asked God to guide him through the ramifications of those mistakes.

Thirty minutes later, they arrived at the townhome he'd shared with Ronnie for six of the last seven years, not as a married couple, yet playing the part. Now innocent Evie bore the fallout of that sin.

"Beating yourself up again?" Dad parked in front of the home, his gaze straight ahead.

Kyle just shook his head. "I'm good at that."

"Well, you can't change the past, but you can learn from it and affect the future. Your choice."

His choice. He inhaled a deep breath and let it out slowly. "I choose to be the best father I can for Evie, regardless of the circumstances."

"See, you're already doing better than I did." Dad opened the truck door.

"You didn't..." But the door had closed behind Dad

before Kyle could get out the dishonest words. His dad hadn't done his best, and they both knew it. So now they were both learning from the past and making better choices going forward.

Kyle got out of the pickup and jogged to catch up to his dad, who was still in great shape for someone in his late fifties. He knocked on the door just in case Ronnie had changed her mind and stuck around. Hearing nothing, he unlocked the door.

They stepped inside, and Kyle once again had to tamp down his frustration. His meager belongings had been piled haphazardly in the middle of the living room, which was bare of other furniture. The supplies for painting the home were stacked against the wall. Ronnie had volunteered to take on the responsibility for selling the home once she got married. She must be getting a head start on the makeover that would silence the bold colors they'd used in each room, removing all the personality from the home.

It's no longer yours, he had to remind himself. *Choose joy.* In planning the worship services going forward, he'd make sure they chose songs of joy.

"Guess they made the moving easy for us." Not exactly joyful, but it was looking at the situation positively, right?

"Guess so." Dad aimed for the crib, the only piece of furniture, in back of the pile. "Let's get this in first, and pack the rest around it.

"Good plan." Together they hefted the crib Ronnie didn't want. Her fiancé had purchased a designer one instead, as if Evie cared. Good for them.

They carried it out to the pickup, and surrounded it with blankets Dad had brought from home, and secured it with bungie straps. Once satisfied that it wasn't going anywhere, they carried the boxes into the home and began packing the remnants of Kyle's life with Ronnie. A notebook full of song ideas. Sheet music. Pictures he'd printed out of Evie. Books for both him and Evie. Bathroom and kitchen supplies that no longer fit Ronnie's style.

Within a couple hours, everything was boxed up and secured in the back of the pickup, all without incident. He could finally go to his new home and start life afresh.

He got in the pickup beside his dad and let that thought wash over him. God had forgiven him and was giving him the fresh start he didn't deserve. Mercy.

"Uh-oh. Trouble's here."

What?

He opened his eyes just as a Mercedes sedan pulled up beside the pickup.

Ronnie and the fiancé. Trouble with a capital T.

Chapter Two

efinitely trouble, unless Evie was with them, then that would be cause for joy.

Kyle opened the pickup door, as did his father.

"This is my mess, Dad. You don't have to get involved."

"When it concerns my son and granddaughter, I'm stepping in."

Okay. "Can't say I didn't warn you."

They both got out of the truck as Ronnie and Mr. Brain Doc—Kyle's favorite nickname for the man—stepped out of their Mercedes.

Kyle walked around the front of the truck while Ronnie stood straight, her hands on her hips, her nose raised high enough to run out of oxygen. Since meeting Mr. Brain Doc, she'd become haughty. Or maybe she'd always been that way, and he hadn't noticed because he was too busy feeding his own vanity.

"I thought you'd be gone already." Ronnie slammed her door. "We left everything nice and easy for you."

Kyle snorted. "Yeah, dumped in a pile. Gee, thanks."

"Nothing was broken."

God, please restrain my tongue from saying something I'll regret. Kyle clenched his hands, focusing his agitation in his palms. "That's true. We got it all packed and are out of your hair." He squinted, checking the backseat of the vehicle for Evie.

"We left her with Gamma, so we can get painting done."

"Well, have a big time." He stuffed down his disappointment and his attitude. If he wanted Ronnie to see what real faith in Jesus looked like, he had to change his mindset toward her, starting now. He relaxed his stance and lifted his frown, though it nearly took a crane to raise it flat. "Give Evie a hug for me, okay?"

Then to Mr. Brain Doc he said, "I appreciate you loving Evie." Which he did. If his daughter was going to spend half her life with father number two, Kyle needed to know Evie was cherished in both homes.

The man nodded and aimed for the house, probably eager to get out of the line of fire.

"There's something else I want to ask you." Ronnie smiled.

But he didn't trust it. "Okay."

"Um, I was looking ahead at the calendar and realized that Evie will be with you on my birthday. Obviously, we should have her then."

We should. She didn't ask, just told him. He opened his mouth to retort, and felt a hand on his shoulder. To further calm his response, he pulled out his phone and brought up his calendar. Interesting. If he wanted to be a jerk, he could be, but this was that opportunity to show he'd changed, even if it hurt as if someone was pinching his heart.

"We can arrange that." He forced out the words.

And her eyes grew as big as guitar picks. "You can?"

"It's only right, as long as I get her on my birthday."

She moved toward him as if to hug him.

No way was that happening, so he stepped back. "Is that all? We want to get going to set up my place."

She shook her head, and her nose angled up toward the clouds. "Fine. We'll see you in about two weeks."

He nodded as he rounded the pickup. When he got inside, a string of words he rarely used punctuated the air like a flat guitar riff. Then he lowered his head and begged for forgiveness. How many times a day would he have to do that?

With his head bowed, he heard the truck start and felt it back down the driveway. Miles flew by before he looked up and watched them pass beneath I-494, heading south on I-35.

"I'm sorry," Dad said so softly, Kyle wondered if he'd heard correctly. "It's a rotten thing she's putting you and Evie through."

That was one way to put it.

"But I'm proud of the way you handled it. I doubt I'd have been as kind."

"It was your calming hand on my shoulder that did it."

Dad laughed. "That hand was there so I didn't punch something."

"Oh." Kyle laughed too. "Guess God can use anything."

"Yes, yes He can." Dad's face grew serious. "Even the broken relationship between a son and father."

Yes, even that.

Be bold and sassy. Stephenie Winter gave herself the pithy pep talk while setting her phone to record. For some reason, speaking to a world of people via her vlog was so much easier than speaking in person. No sweats, no shakes, no panic attacks. Maybe because the audience wasn't right in front of her. Or maybe because she had the power to edit out mistakes.

Regardless, her vlog, *Be Bold & Sassi*, had taken off without a bit of marketing from her. Apparently, a lot of single—and even married—women needed the encouragement nowadays.

She still did.

But this vlog was helping.

Today, while walking through the neighborhood park, she planned to expound on the outdated tradition of bouquet throwing. Even though she'd turned that event into something empowering, she wouldn't be at all upset if the ritual went the way of the dowry.

She set the video to face herself, pasted on a smile. One rule of thumb for vlogging was to be still, but her followers enjoyed walking along with her and didn't mind the shaky cam. Go figure.

She hit "record" as she began walking the park path. "Be bold, ladies!" She imagined women in the audience shouting back, "Be bold," while thrusting their fists into the air. That always compelled her to keep going. "And be Sassi!" Again, she left a couple of beats for the audience to respond before she continued.

"This past weekend I attended my brother's wedding. Though it was her first marriage, and Daniel's second, it was still a small outdoor affair—yes, even with the rain!— with a handful of friends and family in attendance followed by a backyard reception. It really was lovely, except..."

She quieted and stopped walking to emphasize the pause.

"Except for that wretched bouquet toss tradition." She resumed her walk at a quicker pace, walking past a playground filled with kids enjoying the lovely May afternoon. "And, yes, guess who they threw the bouquet to even though I wasn't playing. Ladies, we do not need a husband to have worth!"

Something she hoped she'd be able to drill into her nieces' heads.

"But let me back up a bit before then, because there was also a victory at this wedding. My uncle, who I dreaded talking to because he loved to goad me about being a spinster." She shivered just saying that word. "Yes, I used that ugly word." Once again, she stopped walking for emphasis. "Tell me, why are single guys called bachelors and women spinsters? Or old maids? And why is it a negative when women remain single? I thought we lived in the twenty-first century. And the term bachelorette is way too reminiscent of that horrible TV series."

She walked toward a pond. "Anyway, my uncle approached me and said he'd been watching the vlog. Yes, my old-fashioned uncle! And he told me I was doing a good job. I swear I was struck dumb by his compli—"

Goosebumps broke out on her arms and heebie-jeebies skittered up her spine, silencing her. She slammed to a stop and paused the video, intuition warning her something was very wrong.

Her gaze scoured the park, from the playground filled with toddlers, to the wooded area the walking path disappeared into, to straight ahead along the path.

There. Seated on a bench not far from her was an older man, probably someone her father's age. He had his phone out, and it was aimed across the pond at the children. *Don't overreact. It could be anything.* Her kid brother the cop's words played through her thoughts, helping her put on the brakes. But she felt it in her bones, that this wasn't innocent. Hadn't Daniel said on Saturday that he wished people would get involved?

Be bold, the words repeated in her head as she fumbled with her phone. It leaped from her hands and hit the blacktop walkway. Her fingers shaking, she bent to pick it up, praying it wasn't broken, and heaved a sigh when she found it intact. She could hear Daniel's voice in her head telling her to take in a slow breath to calm the jitters as she scrolled through her contacts to find the number for the local police department.

To think she'd scoffed at Daniel when he'd added it to her contacts.

The phone rang a couple of times before someone answered, "Northfield Police."

"This is Stephenie Winter, and I'd like to report a possible child stalker."

She spent the next minutes talking to them, describing what she saw, while she kept an eye on the man from a distance. Daniel would never forgive her if she approached the creep. When she hung up, she sat on a bench close enough to monitor the guy without him getting suspicious of her. She hoped. She also trained her phone on him, with a quick scan from him to across the pond where kids played and parents chatted among themselves, oblivious to the man's actions.

He sat there, his phone directed at them, his lips moving, his voice inaudible. If she were still a praying woman, she'd ask for the protection for the children, for speedy arrival of the police.

What seemed like too many minutes later, she finally spotted a couple of officers approach the man, and she started the video again. The man startled and tried to break away, but they forced him to sit. He argued, clutching his phone close to his chest, before reluctantly handing it over. He then bowed his head, probably from shame.

She lauded herself for being bold and calling it in, but had she done enough? Gnawing on her lower lip, she looked down at her phone and replayed the video she'd taken of him. She'd gotten a good closeup of the creep so that anyone who saw him in the street could recognize him. He even looked a bit familiar to her. No doubt because she'd passed him before on one of her jogs.

Chills invaded her body.

People needed to know, now, there was a stalker in their neighborhood, and not wait until they read it in the local paper next week.

And she had just the audience to share it to.

She hurried home, spliced together her vlog and the video of the man, and hit "Publish." She shared the vlog on the neighborhood website, then to every other social media outlet she was a member of.

That man would never again harm an innocent child.

Kyle tapped his foot on the church's library/conference room floor. Weekly staff meetings were always the worst part of his job. And in this new church comprised mostly of people his dad's age and older, a lot of the congregation was stuck in their ways.

Of course, he'd learned too late that wasn't necessarily a bad thing.

His phone vibrated in his pocket, informing him he had a message. His hand reached for the phone then stopped. Crazy how habitual it had become to answer right away. The previous church he'd been at had a leadership team all in their thirties and younger and no one thought it rude to check their phones in the middle of a meeting.

The first time he'd checked his phone here during the middle of a meeting, the secretary had skewered him with a look that would have had Thor shaking in his Asgardian boots. Kyle only needed to be skewered once.

His phone buzzed again. Probably Ronnie upset with him that he hadn't responded immediately. Tough. He had other priorities now. Even if this meeting was dreary, and mostly didn't pertain to him.

"Kyle, any changes to the music on Sunday?"

Finally, his turn on the agenda. He pulled out his notebook with all his suggestions. "Just one. For the opening hymn, I'd like to substitute 'Amazing Grace.'" Dad had said he might come this Sunday, and Kyle wanted to make the best impression possible. No one objected to the change, which wasn't a surprise. They could probably sing the beloved hymn every week, and the congregation wouldn't tire of it.

"During offering, the choir will be singing the John Rutter version of 'For the Beauty of the Earth.' This piece was also done by Michaelson." He added that tidbit to appease the board. The previous worship pastor, who'd been loved by all it seemed, had left a huge conducting baton for Kyle to yield.

"And the closing song is '10,000 Reasons.' That's a perfect way to send out the congregation." Periodically, he snuck in a more contemporary song. Sometimes church members liked what he chose, but other times he received plenty of negative feedback. This song had been popular on the radio a few years back, so hopefully most were familiar with it.

"I like that one." The church president weighed in. "It might appeal to some of our youth."

Kyle held in a chuckle. If that was what he thought the youth were listening to, he was way out of touch.

"I like it." Pastor Mitch scribbled something in his notes.

"How's the music budget looking for the summer?" the president asked as Kyle's phone buzzed again. Now that was strange, but he still resisted looking. Ten more minutes and they'd be done here.

"Kyle?"

What? He blinked and looked to the president. "Sorry. I..." *Tell the truth.* "I was distracted by some other thought." And just like that his phone buzzed again. "I'm sorry, I have to look at this." He pulled out his phone. "Someone's been buzzing me the last several minutes, and now I'm concerned."

Without waiting for approval, Kyle hurried from the conference room to the church lobby before checking his messages. Four. From Dad?

He jabbed his dad's name and read the string of messages:

> *– Call me –*
> *– Did you get my message? –*
> *– I think I'm in trouble –*
> *– I'm at the police station –*

What? No way. Kyle hit the call button next to Dad's name. Dad might not be perfect, but Kyle couldn't imagine what he'd be arrested for.

"About time you called." There was the gruff man Kyle had grown up with.

"I'm sorry. I was in a meeting. We're not allowed…" Why was he explaining. "What's going on?"

His dad's silence was punctuated by the board members leaving the library.

"Dad?"

"I don't know." His voice shook. "Someone's accused me of something awful. The police took the phone. I didn't do it, Kyle. I'd never do something like that."

"Wait, what? If the police took your phone, how are you talking to me?"

"Not my phone. Your mom's."

"Mom's phone?" None of this was making any sense.

"Yes, it has the video."

What video? Kyle shook his head. Didn't matter. His dad needed him. Now. He'd find out more later.

"I'll be right there." Kyle hung up and spun around, almost slamming into Pastor Mitch.

"Something we can pray about?"

"I don't—" have the time, was about to come out of his mouth, but now prayer was even more important. "Yes." He waved the other board members to come close. He tried to keep his voice even, but fear still shook it. "My dad's in trouble. I don't know what kind, but he's at the police station and is scared to death."

Pastor Mitch laid his hand on Kyle's shoulder, and then other hands were braced on his arms and back as the pastor prayed aloud. "Lord, You know what's going on here. Ray is in trouble and he needs Your help. Give him and Kyle Your peace. Give the police wisdom and common sense and reveal the truth to them. In Your holy name, Jesus. Amen."

"Thank you," he whispered, holding back tears he couldn't define. The love spilling through the pastor's words and the board members' hands wasn't something he'd ever experienced in his past ten years at True North, his previous church. These people really cared. Really believed. And their prayers were not going to bounce back.

"I'll keep you all posted." He rushed out to his car and was buckled before he realized he'd left his guitar in the church. No matter. He knew where it was, and getting to his dad quickly was more important. He knew what happened when he didn't put his parents first.

He started the vehicle and began driving out of his parking spot, then realized he had no clue where the police station was. He was relatively new to the area and that certainly wasn't a place he frequented.

After programming the address into his GPS, he pulled onto the road and pushed past the speed limit. If the cops pulled him over, well, guess he'd get a personal escort.

Ten long minutes later he arrived. He bolted inside and aimed for the receptionist.

"Kyle."

"Dad?" He swiveled to his right so quickly, he lost his balance. He splayed his hand on the wall to keep from falling. Dad sat in a chair in the reception area. So, did that mean he wasn't under arrest?

His father got up and walked toward him, his slow gait and hunched shoulders aging him twenty years.

Dad gripped Kyle's arm and spoke in a near whisper. "Let's go."

Not wanting to argue or make a scene here, he followed his dad out of the station and into his crossover before beginning the conversation.

"What's going on?"

Dad just grunted.

Kyle took that as a signal to head home. Maybe Dad would feel more comfortable talking about it there. Respecting his father's wishes, Kyle remained silent on the drive. No singing, humming, nothing. In twenty minutes, they arrived at the twin home and Dad trudged toward his unit. Kyle followed even when Dad looked back and give him a 'Don't follow me' death glare.

As if that would stop him.

He barged into his dad's side of the home as Dad grumbled more while slouching down into his recliner. The man obviously didn't feel like talking, but no way was Kyle going to leave him alone.

"Can I get you something? Coffee? Something to eat?"

"Not hungry."

Okay. Kyle understood that. When Ronnie had left him, taking their unborn daughter, food was the last thing on his mind.

"Then how about a game of cards? Checkers?" Dad loved

chess, but Kyle was clueless when it came to strategy games.

"Do you know what day it is?"

So, the man talked. Kyle sat on the couch adjacent to Dad's chair and considered the date. It was Tuesday. May... May 5... Oh no, it was Mom and Dad's anniversary! No wonder he was down. Mom had died before Mother's Day last year, so this was Dad's first anniversary alone. If Kyle did his math correct, this year they would have celebrated forty years together.

"I'm sorry." He finally eked out. "Would this have been forty?"

Dad just nodded.

"I'm sorry," he said again, and he was. He missed Mom too. She'd always been in his corner, even when Dad hadn't. But missing Mom didn't answer all of Kyle's questions, mainly, what happened that brought Dad to the police station?

How did Kyle broach that topic with sensitivity, especially on a day like today?

Maybe the best help was just being here, lifting his dad in prayer.

He sat back on the couch, opened up his palms, and welcomed in God by being still and silent. He'd often struggled with listening to others, so this was one way God had instructed him to pray.

"I did nothing wrong," his dad broke the long silence.

Kyle lifted his gaze toward his father, remaining mute, hoping that would compel Dad to speak.

He sniffled. "All I was doing was watching a video of your mother and I, the one you recorded on your mom's phone of the two of us singing, 'You are My Sunshine.'"

Kyle nodded and allowed a smile at the memory. Even though his dad wasn't the best singer, when he and Mom had sung together, harmonized together, nothing sounded more beautiful.

"I was watching that video, with your mom's phone, while sitting on our favorite park bench. It was the closest I could get to her today, and then..." He sniffled.

"It's okay, Dad, you don't have to say more."

"But I do." Dad's sorrow filled eyes connected with Kyle's. "Someone said I was filming, stalking young children. Why would they accuse me of doing something so awful?"

Daniel closed his eyes, envisioned the scene at the park, and could see how someone would misinterpret. "But Mom's phone was proof, right? You weren't arrested, were you?" That was probably a stupid question, but he didn't know how any of that worked.

Dad shook his head. "They looked at her phone and mine. Said the accuser made a mistake."

"Well, you're home now. You're free." Still, Kyle could see how such an ugly accusation would be jarring. What his dad needed now was something to take his mind off the incident, and Kyle knew exactly what that was. "There's a baseball game on tonight, isn't there?"

"Since when do you like baseball?" His gruff tone was one Kyle remembered from his youth.

"Since you need someone to watch it with. I know the basics, and I'll root for the guys wearing blue, white, and red."

Dad harrumphed.

At least he didn't object. Kyle checked his watch. An hour until game time. That would give him plenty of time to pick up supper. "You still like Main Street Pizza, don't you?"

Finally, light returned to his father's eyes. "Still the best." The pizza had been the family favorite when Kyle was young.

"Pepperoni?"

"Extra pepperoni."

"Got it." Kyle took out his phone and placed the order for pizza and mozzarella sticks online. "I'll be right back." He got up and headed for the front door.

"Thanks, son."

Kyle looked back and smiled at his dad, though anger surged through him at whoever would make such insidious accusations. Tonight, he'd do whatever he could to erase the ugly memory and replace it with good ones.

The drive only took fifteen minutes, but the pizza wouldn't be ready for another fifteen, so he sat and killed time by scrolling through social media as conversations from other pizza lovers swirled around him.

"Did you see the *Be Bold & Sassi* vlog today?" One woman said as she bounced a child on her lap.

"I did." The other woman responded with a nasally voice. "Can you believe there are sickos like that in our town?"

A warning flair went off in Kyle's mind as he looked

toward the two women.

"Right? Who films kids at the park? That's just scary."

No. They couldn't be talking about Dad, could they? What was the vlog they were talking about?

Tension coursing through his veins, he leaned toward them to make conversation. "What is this you're talking about? I've got a one-year old daughter," he added to justify his interest.

"It's all over social media. It's gone viral." The woman with the whiny child said. "I've shared it everywhere. People need to know about creeps like this in our town."

"I agree." Kyle managed to say. "But what was the vlog you mentioned? I haven't heard of it before."

She laughed. "Well, that's 'cause you're a man."

Seriously? He was ready to strangle the name out of her, but he maintained his cool. Mostly. "And I'm a father who's concerned about my daughter."

"No need to get upset." She set her wiggly toddler on the floor. Gross. "Check out the *Be Bold & Sassi* vlog. She even got video of the loser."

A video of him? Oh, no. "I'll do that." He swallowed back bile. "Thanks."

His fingers fumbled over the phone keys as he tried typing in the vlog title. Finally, it came up and the top item was a video.

Of his dad. The bile clawed up his throat. He held down the volume button, silencing it for now, and then the video spun from the man and a different face appeared on the screen.

And iced his veins.

It couldn't be, could it?

The woman's face was familiar, yet thinner than the woman he used to date. And this woman's hair was short, sassy like the vlog name suggested. Trip's hair had been long, thick, and wavy. Trip had the biggest heart he'd ever seen in someone.

Until he'd shattered it in a zillion tiny pieces.

This couldn't be her. She would never do this to anyone. Would she?

Nah. She was terrified of attention, of speaking or singing in front of others, and the vlog had a much larger audience than their church had.

Still...

Well, there was one way to find out. He held his breath as he scrolled through the vlog, looking for a name, but his fingers that picked intricate melodies on the guitar forgot how to work. The ice in his veins must have frozen his brain as well and everything connected to it.

There. The *About Me* tab. Holding his breath, he tapped the button, and a different picture filled the screen, a different angle of the woman who looked even more like Trip. He scrolled down, and his heart stopped pumping.

The vlogger *was* Trip, or what most people knew her as, Stephenie Winter.

A surge of anger thawed his veins and his brain.

Was this retribution for what he'd done to her years ago?

Didn't matter. Once he found her, she was going to be sorry that she ever spread those horrific lies about his father.

Chapter Three

Steph sat down with her guitar as she watched the views for her vlog rise higher than anything she'd ever posted before. This was the power of media in the technology age. No more children would be threatened by this man. One more creep off the streets.

She deserved a night off for this. Usually she spent the evenings as a rideshare driver, but she was taking the night off. She loved the freedom of being her own boss. The job brought in the money she needed to pay for her daily needs, while allowing her to pursue her artistic passions. If this video kept getting hits, she might even make a dollar or two off of it. But that certainly wasn't her intent. Getting a bad guy off the street was.

Closing her eyes, she picked out a new melody on her guitar. A feel-good melody, one worth keeping. So, she penciled in notes and chords on music paper as the song developed in her heart and flowed to her brain. This was the most inspired she'd been in months. Usually, lyrics came first.

Back when she and Jerkwad had dated, they'd made a great team with him pouring out beautiful tunes that fit her lyrics perfectly.

Why did she think of him now? It had been years since he'd skittered through her mind like that big, black spider that scurried across her studio wall yesterday. She shivered just thinking about it. If only Jerkwad's face was as easy to flush as that spider had been.

She strummed her guitar and grimaced. Definitely not that chord. She tried another and nodded. That worked.

Her phone sang out her text tune, and she jumped. Why hadn't she shut it off?

She checked the message. Angie!

> *— Saw your vlog today.*
> *You go, girl! —*

For her best friend, Steph would take a break. She set aside her guitar and texted back.

> *— Can you believe it?*
> *He was filming kids,*
> *right there in the open! —*

> *— Gave me the chills.*
> *Thanks for being bold and sassy —*

> *— That's Sassi! —*

> *— Ha ha.*
> *What are you up to tonight?*

*Want to grab a drink to celebrate
your vlogging success? –*

*– Absolutely.
Give me an hour to freshen up. –*

– Cranby's? –

– See you there at seven. –

She wasn't stupid enough to drive herself, just in case she had a drink too many. Daniel would never let her live it down. Nor would her sisters. Or parents. But none of them knew how to have fun.

So, she arranged for a ride then hurried to her bathroom and freshened up. She loved this new, short hairstyle that allowed her to just wet, scrunch, and run. Oh, and look fabulous along with sassy. After refreshing her makeup for a night-out look, she put on skinny jeans, a black tank, and a sparkly jacket. She topped off the outfit with a pair of Converse sneakers. Being tall, she and heels didn't get along. Besides, tennies were far more comfortable to dance in. Once dressed, she stood in front of the long mirror hung on the living room side of her bathroom door.

She looked good, if she did say so herself. No doubt, she wouldn't have any trouble finding a dance partner tonight. Amazing how the right haircut and outfit could build confidence.

The driver was on time, so she left him a healthy tip

when he dropped her off. Paying goodness forward was always a smart idea.

The music inside Cranby's thumped outside the building so much so that she almost anticipated the walls would fall like Jericho. Well, if they did, she'd be sure to catch it for her vlog. She squeezed among the crowds and found Angie at their normal table, right in the middle of the ruckus. There was a time when Steph would have hated that and begged to find a table off in a quiet corner, but that Stephenie Winter had died right along with her relationship with Jerkwad. Never would that skittish woman see the light of day again.

She sat across from Angie, who pushed a drink her way.

"Try this." Angie shouted to be heard. "It's amazing."

"What is it?" Steph shouted back. Angie was always trying new drinks, and half were horrible. Steph had learned to get the details before sipping.

"It's an Old Fashioned—whiskey, bitters, orange rind, and topped with a maraschino cherry—so I know you'll like it."

Steph sipped and her taste buds agreed with Angie. She gave her the thumbs-up.

Angie showed two thumbs-up which conveyed something else entirely: cute men were approaching, which meant tonight was off to a great start.

A couple of guys came up to the table. Angie was right, they were very nice looking.

The taller of the two, with the hair-shaved-on-the-side-and-long-on-top look, grinned at Steph then Angie. Reminded her of a certain over-slick worship pastor she'd once known. "Buy you ladies a drink?"

Instead of answering, Steph just sipped at her drink.

"Of course." Angie answered for them, as Steph knew she would. Unlike Angie, Steph never liked to look too eager.

"Hey, aren't you the Sassi lady?" one of the guys asked.

She quickly hid her smile at being recognized for the first time in public. "Maybe I—"

"You bet she is." Angie talked over her.

"Well." Without invitation, the hair guy pulled out a chair and sat down. "Pleased to meet you, Sassi lady."

Already, she didn't like him. And the man's breath gave away that he'd had his share of drinks already. Not the kind of guy she needed to get involved with, even for an evening.

"Tony, let them be." The friend looked exasperated with his buddy.

"What?" Tony splayed his hands. "I just offered to buy them a drink."

"Now." The friend jerked his thumb over his shoulder.

"Whatever." Tony stood up and grinned down at Steph. "If you change your mind…"

She intentionally rolled her eyes, hoping he'd catch the hint. He just sashayed away, probably stalking his next victim. She shivered at that.

"Hey, I'm sorry about Tony." The guy's friend looked over his shoulder. "My kid brother thinks he's God's gift. To what? I don't know. Tonight, I have the dubious distinction of being his designated driver."

"What we do for our siblings, right?" Steph might not

always agree with them, but she'd always stand up for them and vice versa.

He just shook his head. "You two have a good evening." He turned and searched the bar.

"I can't believe you sent him away!" Angie leaned across the table. "Would have saved us some money."

"And cost us a whole bunch of grief." Unlike the dude's brother. Now that was the kind of guy she could spend time with.

"Well, if you're not interested..." Angie got up and squeezed through the crowd toward the jerk.

"I see you've been ditched, too." The brother was back, which was just fine.

"I'm used to it." She pointed toward Angie's seat.

"Actually, I was thinking of taking a page from Tony's book." He gestured toward the crowded dance floor and shrugged. "Um, you wouldn't want to kill some time dancing, would you?"

"I would love to, but I need to know who I'm dancing with."

"Oh." He scratched the back of his neck. Man, the dude was shy, just like she used to be. "I'm Rod."

"Nice to meet you, Rod." She extended her hand, letting him help her up. "When people aren't calling me Sassi Lady, I go by Stephenie."

"Pleased to meet you, Stephenie." He gestured for her to take the lead. So far, he was the perfect gentleman. How had he ended up with a brother like Tony?

As she walked toward the dance floor, her phone vibrated. Whoever it was could wait. They danced to a couple of '80s rock tunes, her phone buzzing a few more times. She ignored each one. Then the music changed to a slow dance. With strangers, she normally wasn't comfortable, but Rod, he seemed different.

"Would you mind?" He offered his hand.

And she took it. He pulled her close, but not tight, again being the perfect gentleman. Her phone sang out her oldest sister's ringtone, that "Sisters" song from *White Christmas*, and he backed away.

"You need to get that?"

She sighed. "I'll get rid of her." By the time she got her phone out of her pocket, Carrie had hung up, but Steph checked the messages. Two from Carrie, and two from Ginny, plus a voice mail from Carrie.

"I'm sorry." She stepped away from Rod. "But I need to see what's going on. Can I take a rain check?"

"Sure thing." He gave a little bow. "Thanks for the dances."

"Thank you." She smiled and turned away and aimed for an open table in a private corner. There, she brought up the messages, one at a time.

– Call me! – (Carrie)

– Mom just got the strangest call – (Ginny)

– I know you're busy partying,
but trust me, you want to talk to me – (Ginny)

– One name: Kyle – (Carrie)

That *one name* made her feel as if she'd just woken up from a night of heavy drinking. What was the problem? Was he sick? Why did he need her now after ten years of silence? Hopefully, the voice mail would answer her questions.

"Hey, Steph, Mom got a strange call from that music guy you used to date. Kyle something or other. Says he needs to talk to you asap." She gave his number then said to call her back.

Those same questions she'd pondered a second ago pestered her brain. Why did he need her? Urgently? If she didn't have to report back to her family—something he'd insured would have to happen by going through her mom. That alone made her angry with him.

To be honest, she'd never stopped being angry with him, and with how he'd ruined her life, she swore she never would.

She searched the bar for Angie and found her glued to Tony. Chances were, Angie wouldn't have a clue if Steph stepped outside for a moment, so once again, she threaded her way through the crowd to the door leading outside.

Brisk air greeted her, along with silence. Per Daniel's instructions, her head was on a constant swivel, making sure she was aware of her surroundings, as she dialed the number Carrie had left for her. It rang three times and she began to hope no one would answer, that this was all a late April Fools' prank.

"Hello."

Her gut lurched at the sound of his voice, relatively

unchanged from ten years earlier. And suddenly, that insecure child Steph had banished years ago took over, and she couldn't get words out.

"Someone there? Trip?"

Anger at the nickname bolted her from her self-doubt. "The name is Stephenie."

"Yeah. Sorry."

Silence occupied the phone line, and she refused to evict it.

"I need to see you."

She laughed at that. "Well, maybe, I don't want to see you."

"I get it." He sighed. "But this is important. It's about my dad."

She closed her eyes and leaned against the bar's brick façade. Kyle hadn't had a good relationship with his father. The man hadn't appreciated Kyle's musical gifts—thought he should have been an athlete instead—which was laughable. Yet, the man had liked her, and she'd developed a soft spot for the gruff-spoken man.

"Is he okay?"

"In the way you're thinking, he's fine. It's something else. And I need to speak to you in person."

"I don't really have time." For him, anyway. She had time for many other people, though.

"Just give me a half hour tonight."

"Tonight?" She laughed out loud at that. "You think I have time for you? I have a life you know."

"Well so do I, and so did my dad." Imagine that, she'd made him angry. Tough. "And I know you live in the

Northfield area, so you're close to me."

He lived near her? The last she'd heard he was still the worship leader for the church they'd once attended together, and that was north of Minneapolis.

Voices neared her, and she realized she was breaking one of Daniel's rules to always be aware of her surroundings. She opened her eyes and clutched the mace attached to her jeans, just in case. A couple, with no space between them, walked past her, seemingly oblivious to anyone or anything around them.

Just like she'd been a moment ago. How easy it was to let down your guard and be injured by someone waiting to swoop in.

Like Kyle had been. She was perfectly justified by refusing to meet him, but something, conscience, intuition, guilt—nah—but something encouraged her to give in.

"You still there, Tri..., I mean, Stephenie?"

"Okay, I'll meet you." She looked up the block at a Denny's. "I'll be at the Denny's in Apple Valley."

"I'll see you there in thirty minutes."

Ha. More like forty-five. He functioned on artist time, which was never early. And that would give her just enough time for another drink or two. She needed that to face Kyle again. And maybe she could use that rain check for a slow dance with Rod.

She tucked away her phone and went back inside the cacophonous bar. Angie was still plastered against Tony. Rod had found himself a new slow dance partner, and they were glued tighter than Tony and Angie, if that was possible.

So, he'd turned out to be just another jerk. Figured.

She had no more reason to stick around here, so she caught Angie's eye and made a motion that she was leaving. Angie gave her a thumbs-up then continued swaying with her dance partner.

Tonight had started out so fun.

She hurried from the bar and tuned her eyes and ears to the sights and sounds of the night. A block wasn't far to walk safely, but she knew what happened when you let your guard down.

With her head on a constant swivel, she made it to Denny's safely then requested a corner booth in the mostly-empty restaurant.

Now what?

She pulled out her phone and checked her vlog stats again. Number of views was still going up, and the rate of rise wasn't slowing. Comments were all encouraging. Many praised her for sharing the video. With her about to face the man who'd taken advantage of her at a vulnerable time, she needed all the good news she could get. If she were still a praying woman, she'd plead for help and wisdom right now in dealing with the man who'd squashed her faith.

Kyle stopped outside the Denny's entry and whispered, "Lord, keep me calm." He'd uttered those same words probably a hundred times since he'd spoken with Pastor

Mitch. When Kyle had called Mitch, he hadn't withheld his anger and disgust at what Trip had done. Thankfully, the pastor had talked Kyle down and encouraged him to view the scene from her perspective. He didn't like it, but it made sense.

And then Mitch had advised Kyle to pray continuously on his way to meet up with Trip, and it had helped temper his anger.

He tugged open the door, stepped inside, and was heartened by the scent of comfort food. Hopefully, by the time he was done meeting with Trip, he'd still have an appetite. The restaurant had two separate seating areas, and he scanned both before landing on a booth in the corner.

Anger built in him, and he tamped it down. Pointing fingers would only make her defensive and would help no one, so he heaved in a breath and slowly let it out as he approached the booth.

"Hey Trip, er, Stephenie." Figured, he messed up already.

Her gaze measured him, and her eyes widened. "Kyle?"

"Mind if I have a seat?"

"You're the one who set up this meeting."

The obvious smell of alcohol reached across the table as he sat. The Steph he remembered wouldn't touch the stuff, but a lot could happen in ten years. He was proof.

He managed a smile, hoping to start the conversation on a good note. "You look great."

"And you look different."

"I'm sure I do." After leaving his old church where hipsters reigned and a worship minister had to look the part, he just wanted to be normal. "Keeping up with trends is exhausting. I just want to be me."

"Words I never thought I'd hear you say."

"Yeah." He chuckled dryly. "You and me both."

She folded her hands around her cup of coffee, and sat up straight, clearly taking charge of the situation. Another change from the Trip he remembered. "I really don't want to go down memory lane. Just tell me what's so important that it couldn't wait."

He mimicked her posture. *Lord, help me keep my calm.*

"Can I get you anything, sir?" The waitress startled them both.

"Uh, just a Mountain Dew, no ice. And bring the tab right away too."

"Will do."

"Is that vegan?" Steph didn't even attempt to mask her sarcasm as the waitress walked away.

He shrugged. "I don't know. I don't worry about that anymore."

"Oh really." Her half smile showed she didn't believe him, not that she had any reason to, and he didn't have the energy to argue. "Let's cut the chitchat. Why was it so necessary for you to interrupt my evening?"

Because you ruined my dad's life, he wanted to spurt out, but kept his mouth in check. "It's about the video you—"

"Vlog."

"Whatever. The one you released today."

"You're upset that I'm having some success?"

"At whose expense?"

"Excuse me? The only ones hurt are those kids that creep was videotaping."

He clamped his mouth shut. Anger was a formidable emotion that was difficult to rein in. "Did you even look at the man in your vid, I mean, vlog?"

"Naturally."

"And you didn't recognize him?"

"No. Should I?"

"Your Dew, no ice." This waitress should be a spy, she was so stealthy.

"Wait." Stephenie's eyes went from narrow to as wide as the pancakes this place served. "That was your dad?"

He nodded and took a long swallow of his drink to prevent nasty words from spewing out.

"How could he do that to kids?" Rage filled her face and voice.

He squeezed his fingernails into his palms, focusing the pain there. "The real question is, how did you not consider that Dad is innocent?"

"Really? I watched him, and then the police talked with him."

"Yeah, they did. And they searched the phone and found a video of Mom and him singing together."

"No." She shook her head as if trying to regain control of this conversation, but her shoulders slumped slightly.

"Yes." He leaned toward her, still bridling his true feelings. "Mom and Dad used to walk to that park and sit on that bench together. Yeah, they watched kids. Watched them play." He spat the word. "Mom died last year, and today would have been their fortieth anniversary. Dad was watching a video of them singing together, like they used to do, and then this heaps on top of him."

She seemed to shrink with each word, then she hugged herself, and her gaze no longer met his. "I'm sorry."

He folded his hands below the table and clamped his eyes closed, and once again prayed silently, *Lord, keep me calm.*

Once he'd stilled his emotions, he looked her in the eye.

She quickly looked away.

But that couldn't stop him from delivering his ultimatum. "Your apology will be accepted once you take down the video and issue a formal apology via your vlog to Dad."

"I can do that." Her voice came out small, timid, as he remembered her once being.

"You *will* do that."

She nodded and shook her head. Then her eyes turned all glossy with tears.

An hour ago, he would have loved to see her hurt, but now? God was clearly working on him. He splayed his hands on the table, hoping to show he was open to forgiving her. "I understand how it must have looked. I have a daughter myself, and if some creep..."

"You have a daughter?"

For that, his grin came easily. "Just a year old. Best thing that ever happened to me."

"Then I'm happy for you." She pulled out her phone and did a bunch of swiping. "There, I've pulled down the video, but I can't do anything about the shares."

His mouth twitched. "Well, you did what you had to."

"And I'll film the apology tomorrow morning."

"Thank you." Whew. That went much easier than he'd anticipated, thanks to advice from Pastor Mitch. Now it was time to get home and let Dad know she was making it better. He got up and grabbed the tab. "Good seeing you again, Trip. Hope all goes well for you."

He aimed for the door.

"Are you going to Northfield?"

He turned back toward her. "Yeah, why?"

"Any chance I could get a ride? I took a rideshare up here."

Why would she take a rideshare unless she'd planned on drinking too much? If that was the case, she really had changed.

He shrugged to keep his response neutral. "Guess so."

"Thanks." Her eyes remained averted as she got up.

"No biggie." He gestured for her to take the lead then left a ten-dollar bill on the table. It wasn't the server's fault that they didn't order anything substantial. Quite the attitude change from a couple years ago when he would have patted himself on the back for saving money. What a chump he'd been. No wonder Ronnie had left him for some other guy.

He paid the bill on the way out, then led her to his vehicle. A strange nervousness pinched him as he aimed for the passenger door.

"I am capable of opening my own door," she snapped at him.

"Fine." He backed away and walked around his car, a million questions running through his mind. What do you talk about with an old girlfriend, one who clearly had a chip on her shoulder, one who'd changed considerably since you last saw her? The Trip he'd known wouldn't have dreamed of doing a vlog, preferring to stay in the background. But that was one thing he'd liked about her.

He got into his crossover and started it up. "Tell me where to go."

"Follow Central Ave. going south." Arms wrapped tightly around herself, she focused out the window.

He could take a hint. "Got it." An uneasy silence surrounded them as he pulled onto the road.

What had happened in her life to change her? Over ten years had passed since they'd dated. Since he'd messed up big time. But that was ten years ago, and God had forgiven him.

Maybe he'd yet to forgive himself.

Whoa. Where had that thought come from? He shook it off. God's forgiveness was enough.

But had he ever apologized to her? He drummed a song on his steering wheel as he thought back to their last date that ended in tears. The official breakup hadn't come until a month later. Ronnie came along a month after that.

So, no apology had ever happened. He almost felt like he was on the Alcoholics Anonymous make-amends-to-everyone plan. No, he hadn't been addicted to alcohol, but to attention? Praise? Acceptance? He'd lived for all. Maybe all addictions should follow the same plan to recovery.

Now wasn't the appropriate time to bring that up, but perhaps this event was God's way of reminding Kyle that he had unfinished business to attend to. This was too much of a coincidence, and he'd learned there really wasn't such a thing as a coincidence. Once he dropped her off, he'd make the offer to get together again, but for now, he couldn't tolerate the silence. Even small talk would help.

"So, what have you been up to?"

She shifted in her seat, but that was the only response.

Okay, then, he'd try another tactic. "How's your family?" They'd always been a priority for her.

More silence.

He sighed. Keeping one hand on the steering wheel, he squeezed the tension from his neck and shoulders. "Okay, I get that this vlog stuff is bothering you. You're fixing it, and we'll all go on as normal. You'll never have to see me again."

"You don't really get it, do you?"

So, she does speak. "What don't I get?"

"That when something goes viral, it can't be undone, and I'm afraid that, if your father really is innocent, I've just ruined his life."

Chapter Four

Why hadn't she just kept her mouth shut? Or instead, answered his innocuous questions?

Because worry niggled at her like a bad itch. She spoke up, just like she was supposed to, and now an innocent man's normal life was at stake.

"First of all, he's definitely innocent, and second, you're being a little dramatic, don't you think? You'll make your apology tomorrow, then Dad'll be yesterday's news. I'm not worried. Besides, I've got a team of prayer warriors on this right now."

Oh, that was rich. So, he was still playing the religious card. "Yeah, I remember those prayer warriors"—She made air quotes—"you surrounded yourself with. A bunch of holier-than-though hypocrites."

"I'm not with them anymore," he said softly, unable to mask his regret. "The church I'm with now, they're real. Their faith is authentic. Not only would they see through pretense, they wouldn't be shy about letting me know. Unlike True North." He laughed, and his hands gripped the steering wheel tighter. "True North. Even the name of that church was a lie."

Wow. If she wasn't hearing it directly from his lips, she wouldn't believe he'd said it. Half of his worship team on True North had been paid instrumentalists, who only cared that they received a paycheck for playing on weekends. They were talented, but had little time for God outside of church. He'd claimed that didn't matter, that allowing them to play was his ministry, when in truth, they'd been hired to make him look good.

"Well, that's good news, at least. It wasn't until I left the church that I realized how fake it all had been." Except for weddings and funerals, she hadn't been back to any church since then, because back then, she'd bought into True North's lies. Kyle's lies. Oh, he had looked good. Sounded amazing. And then when he showed interest in quiet little her, she would have done anything for him.

And she had.

She got the shimmies just thinking about how gullible she'd been. If, through her vlog, she could save one insecure woman from giving in to a man's control, all the time spent would be worth it.

But was it worth ruining a man's life over?

If Kyle's dad really was innocent.

Of course, Kyle would defend his father. He hadn't been trustworthy back then, why should she believe him now?

Wow. She bonked her head on the headrest as the truth became clear. Boy, was he a good liar. In talking with Kyle for only a few minutes, she'd fallen back into his trap and believed him without proof. She'd even deleted her post.

Well, that apology she'd promised for tomorrow morning wasn't happening, not until he could prove his dad's innocence, because a child's life was far more important.

She sat up straight in her seat, regaining control of herself and the situation, ignoring his further attempts at small talk. Thankfully, after a few minutes of trying to engage her, he took the hint. The only communication from there on were her simple, "left here," "another left," and "drop me off here." Her anger at his deception and her trusting grew hotter with each mile.

He pulled to the curb of the cute rambler she'd had her eye on for ages. No, it wasn't her home, but he didn't need to know that, and she certainly didn't want him to know where she really lived. That was none of his business.

Remaining tight-lipped, she stepped out of his crossover. She held the door open and looked back at him, piercing him with her glare. "Just an FYI. I figured out your little scheme."

"What are—"

"Yeah, I fell for it at first, but I'm not that naïve little girl you dated ten years ago, and I won't be fooled again."

The last thing she saw before she slammed the door shut was his panic-filled face. Good. He deserved to suffer like she had, and she refused to be taken in by him again.

Kyle stared, gape-mouthed at Trip's striding figure. What

just happened here? She'd believed him, and then seemed to do a one-eighty, suddenly reminding him of that pompous piece-of-work he'd been ten years ago. Would he never be able to shake that off? God had forgiven him, but clearly the world wouldn't let him forget.

And now his actions from years ago were hurting his father today.

He put his vehicle in gear and resisted the urge to squeal away, not wanting to wake anyone this time of night. Instead, he pulled onto the street and aimed for his new home, probably a mere five minutes away. His father was likely sleeping already, which would be a blessing. Kyle didn't want to burden his rest with this.

What was that verse from the Bible? The one about sins affecting third and fourth generations of family? Well, in his case, that meant parents as well as children.

But Kyle now knew Someone who would listen and understand and not be burdened. Someone who would shoulder that burden for him.

In less than five minutes, he arrived at his new home that was still sparsely decorated. If it were just him living here, that wouldn't matter, but he wanted Evie to feel at home when she came. Less than two weeks until he got to see her again, but his heart still ached at the separation.

If his heart felt this painful, imagine how Evie's must feel being shuffled between homes. Pastor Mitch would call that seeing from someone else's perspective, which was what he needed to do with Trip.

He poured himself a glass of water then retired to his

bedroom. The Bible he once highlighted for show, and was now dog-eared from heavy use, sat below the lamp on one of the milk crates he used for bed stands. Tonight, he planned to spend a lot of time in the Word, praying for open eyes, ears, and heart. Asking for wisdom on how to proceed rather than letting his emotions do his thinking and reacting for him, as he'd once done.

He dressed for bed then buried himself in scripture.

When morning sunlight sliced through the crack between his curtains, waking him, his Bible still lay open on his lap. He glanced to his right, and the clock read six twenty-five, a mere five minutes before his alarm would go off. Desiring more rest after a restless night, he wiped a hand down his face, trying to wake it. Didn't work.

Even so, he anticipated having breakfast with his father. They'd just begun a devotional written specifically for fathers and sons that was helping to repair the rift between them. He was finally learning to see things through his father's eyes.

Perspective.

God was slowly teaching Kyle to see the heart that He saw and to see people through Jesus' eyes. Too often, that open-eyed viewpoint was agonizing. No one wants to see how self-absorbed or narrow-minded they've been.

But it was also easier to offer grace when you understood that every person has a backstory that leads to their decisions today. Just like he had. And he appreciated those who took the time to see him through Jesus' eyes.

He showered, then grabbed his Bible and study book. He

hurried over to his dad's side of the home, and knocked before letting himself in.

"Morning." Dad sat at his dining room table, with two cups of coffee and a pan of Johnnie cake, likely made from a box. As long as the cornbread was slabbed with butter, Kyle didn't care if it came from a box or was made from scratch.

"Morning." Kyle set his books on the table then cut himself a large slice of cake.

"You look tired." Dad sipped at his coffee.

"That's because I haven't had coffee yet." Kyle added cream to his then sipped, letting the caffeine jumpstart his system. "And because I had an interesting night."

"Uh-oh."

"I talked with Trip."

Dad set down his cup and stared at it. "I had a feeling."

"The thing is, she was good at first. When I explained what you were doing in the video, she felt bad and even deleted the post. Promised to record an apology. Then I drove her home, and she seemed to be opening up, but the next minute she became an ice queen, treating me as if I were one of her lowly servants. She capped off the evening by accusing me of lying. Again."

"Again?" Dad cut himself more cake, his hand clearly shaking.

"I don't know that I ever outright lied to her, but as you know," he looked down at his coffee cup and swirled around the cream until it blended in, "my behavior wasn't what you'd expect from a music minister, so my title alone was a lie."

"Hmm." Dad kept his gaze down, too.

Kyle's thoughts exactly. "But I'm not giving up. I...you need a formal apology from her to make this right." But first, if he wanted to clear Dad's present, he needed to amend for his personal past, and that meant asking Trip if they could meet somewhere. If she refused, then a phone apology would have to suffice.

"I appreciate that, son."

Son. Such a precious word to him now. He would no longer take it for granted.

He gestured to his Bible and the study guide. "Let's get started."

For the next forty-five minutes, the two read scripture together, prayed together, studied together, just like father and son should. He couldn't change his past, but he could affect their future, and that began with a long-overdue apology. Tonight, following work, he'd contact her again, and he wouldn't give up until she listened.

Following the study, he hurried to work. Today he planned to work on some new music, set up the PowerPoint for Sunday, do some tech stuff, with lunch with Pastor Mitch in between. During the school year, Wednesday evenings were devoted to working with the youth band, something he loved, but last week had been the last youth worship until fall.

Continuing it through summer was another change he hoped to make for next year.

By the time he'd finalized the PowerPoint for Sunday's

service, it was already eleven forty-five. He logged out of his laptop and hurried to meet Pastor Mitch at a local family-owned restaurant that claimed to serve the best burgers in the area. Studying all the mouthwatering options on the menu, he couldn't wait to test that claim, one burger at a time.

"Good afternoon, pastor." A waitress, probably old enough to be his mother, stopped by the table and set glasses with water in front of both of them. "Did you have a good Easter?"

"Couldn't have been better, Jeanie. Someday, I'll even convince you to come sit in the pews." He nodded toward Kyle. "Even got ourselves a new worship minister, one who plans to bring our church into the twentieth century."

Kyle dropped his menu. "Don't you mean twenty-first?"

Pastor Mitch laughed. "One century at a time, please."

"Well." Jeannie tapped a pen against her pad. "If everyone there is as good looking as the two of you, then maybe I'll give it a try. I've heard church dating is a thing."

"Whatever it takes to bring you through those doors."

"It'll happen someday, pastor." She winked at him. "Now what can I get you boys for lunch?"

"Mushroom and swiss burger for me." Mitch handed his menu to Jeanie.

"And you?" She looked at Kyle.

"Do you recommend the macaroni and cheeseburger?"

"Honey, I recommend all our burgers." She patted her ample stomach. "As you can tell, I've sampled them all frequently."

He laughed. "Then that's what I'll have." One other thing that had changed with him since the job switch was that he was no longer being pretentious about the food he liked. At his old church, the cool people were vegetarians or vegans, and he'd gone along for appearances. He was quickly learning how much easier life was when you were true to yourself.

And the truth was, he enjoyed a good hamburger. He just might have to up his workout, though, or he'd be spending his paychecks on a new wardrobe.

After Jeanie walked away, Pastor Mitch leaned toward him, keeping his tone low. "You seem pretty upbeat considering the day you had yesterday."

He did, didn't he? "Is that what happens when you begin the day in the Word?"

"Sometimes, but spending time with God isn't a magic pill that will take all your troubles away."

"I get that."

"I know, but it's a good reminder for both of us."

They made small talk the next few minutes until the burgers arrived. He bit into his, and his eyes rolled back in his head. Okay, he'd definitely be upping his workout.

"I take it, you like it." Pastor dipped a crinkle fry into ketchup.

"That's an understatement."

"I knew you'd like it." Jeanie stopped by to top off their water glasses and coffee cups. "By the way, pastor, have you heard about that horrible man roaming about Northfield?"

Kyle's nerves went on full alert, and he dropped the

burger onto his plate, keeping his gaze straight ahead on the pastor.

"I've heard rumors, Jeanie, but that's all they are." Pastor Mitch gave her his kind and convincing smile. "I happen to know the family of the accused, and the man is innocent."

"Well, if you watch the video, you might change your mind."

Kyle ground his teeth together to avoid saying something he'd regret.

"As a matter of fact, I have seen the video, and I still know the man is innocent."

"Hmph." She turned quicker than a woman her size should be able to and stalked away.

Suddenly, his burger tasted like mud. Just looking at it gave him an upset stomach.

"I'm sorry, Kyle."

"Not your fault," he mumbled through clenched jaws then wiped his mouth with a napkin. He might not make it to tonight before calling Trip.

"No, but it's a maddening situation." Even the pastor threw down his burger. "People spreading rumors always makes my blood boil. Maybe I should change up my sermon for this Sunday."

"I wouldn't be opposed." Kyle wrapped his burger in a napkin to eat later. "In my opinion, churches can be too wishy-washy on issues."

"Is that spoken from experience?"

"Uh-uh. No more counseling sessions today. I just want

to head back to church and pound on the keyboard for a bit.”

“And I’ll do some heavy-duty talking with God. We have to stop this before it grows any further.”

“Dad and I appreciate—”

Kyle’s phone sang Chris Tomlin’s “Amazing Grace,” Dad’s ringtone. He never called during the day.

“Sorry, I have to take this.” He whipped the phone from his pocket and swiped Answer. “Hi Dad.”

All he heard was heavy, quick breathing, followed by a sniffle. “You...they...our house.”

“I’ll be right there.” He swiped the End Call button. He didn’t know what happened, but it had to be bad to leave his father stammering.

“What’s wrong?”

“I don’t know.” He got up and threw a couple of bills on the table, leaving the waitress a far bigger tip than she deserved. “And it scares me to death.”

“Then I’m coming with you.”

“You don’t have to.”

“No, I don’t, but I want to, and I’m driving.”

Kyle didn’t argue, but followed the pastor to his sedan, mindful of the chill that had taken over the air. He prayed the entire ride home, which seemed to take far too long. At last the car slowed and made a sharp turn. Stopped. Turned off.

“Oh boy,” the pastor whispered.

Kyle pried open his eyes, looked up, and his breath caught. Spray painted in red across the front of the townhome were the words, "Child Predator. Leave town or else."

After months of tumbling down life's hill, he'd thought things were going to start climbing upward—he hadn't imagined they could plummet any lower.

But they just had.

Chapter Five

*A*nd that's how you tell your former boyfriends to get lost." Steph recorded on her phone while hunkered down in a booth at her favorite coffee shop. "I know how difficult it can be to speak up sometimes. I was once a naive people-pleaser who didn't want to rock the boat, and that only ended up hurting me. It got me involved with a guy who took advantage of my innocence. So how did I break out of that mold? How did I become a spokesperson for the *Be Bold & Sassi* movement?"

She leaned closer to her phone, filling the screen with her face. "By putting myself in positions that required speaking and required that I not be taken advantage of. Becoming a rideshare driver took care of much of that. I became my own boss. I have to communicate with people and, if I want to make any money, I have to stand up for myself. Having to do this in business has helped me grow tremendously in my personal life."

She backed away from the camera and smirked. "Now, of course, I've taken missteps along the way, done a lot of stupid things—that's for another vlog, ladies!—but I've also learned that I have value. My 'no' means no. And if my conscience or intuition is pricking at me over some situation, I've learned to listen to it."

Her voice grew hoarse from all the talking, so she took a sip of water to lubricate her vocal cords. "I have an assignment for you. Write down what you consider to be your personal weaknesses. What can you do to add muscle to them? Exercising, of course. For me, being a driver exercised my communication muscles. Doing this vlog has toned those muscles. I'd love to hear what you come up with! Next week, I'll share your ideas with my audience. Working together, thinking together, we are all stronger."

She raised her cup of coffee in salute to her audience. "Until next time, stay bold and sassi, ladies!" She ended the video and sat back in the booth, satisfied with another nearly-finished vlog. Just a little bit of editing was required, but her viewers preferred the raw honesty of minimal editing. They also liked seeing her in settings they could easily visualize themselves in, hence the bustling coffee shop location. They even identified with the reality of the bloopers that always appeared in her videos as opposed to finely edited vlogs that came off as airbrushed.

Once she finished her drink, she'd hurry home where she could concentrate on tweaking the video before uploading it to her vlog. After that, the post would be ready to go live. Her fans would really like this one. Too many would identify with having a former boyfriend lying to get something they wanted. They just had to be firm and look past the guy's charisma or whatever it was that made her fall for him in the first place. Women had to learn to stand up for themselves.

She got up from the booth and slung her purse over her shoulder. Once the post went live, she'd be free to do some driving tonight. Her funds were running low, and if she wanted to eat next week, that meant driving this week.

Her phone rang a generic tune as she aimed for the coffee shop door. Generic usually meant a spam call, so she let it go to voice mail. Most hung up before then. The phone pinged, alerting her that whoever had called left a message. She got in her Ford Escape and shut the door before listening.

"Stephenie, I realize you're upset with me, and I get it, and I know 'I'm sorry' doesn't begin to make up for what I did to you, but please don't let this rift between us hurt my dad any further. I know you don't believe he's innocent—I don't know what to do to change your mind about that—but he is innocent, and he's just been threatened. He's scared to death, Trip, and you can help. Please help."

Steph leaned back in her seat and closed her eyes. Oh, he sounded scared, worried, sincere, but that still didn't make him truthful.

But what if his dad was innocent? Was it better to err on his side or the children's? That was a no-brainer. Always care for the children first.

But...

She groaned. *If* he was innocent, then she was guilty of injuring him, and she couldn't bear that burden.

Think, woman, think. Her eyes pinched tight. Wait,

hadn't Kyle said the other night that the police had exonerated him? Well, then, that was the step he needed to take. If Kyle's dad was truly innocent, they'd be able to verify it.

She opened her eyes, started her car, and hit the Call button on her phone. The ring sounded on her Bluetooth over the car speakers.

"Steph?" He still sounded urgent.

But she wasn't about to let down her guard. "You want me to retract what I said on my vlog? Then I need to hear from the police that he's innocent."

Silence followed by whispers. "Sure. Fine. They're on the way here as I speak. Come on over, and you can hear it directly from them."

"Uh-uh. I'm not coming to your place. Instead, ask them to make a video stating your dad's innocence." That was something her brother would do if this had been one of his cases. "*If* your dad isn't guilty, I'll add their video to my apology, then all will be good."

"Think they'll do that?"

"Daniel would."

"Can you call him, ask him for a favor?"

"No can do. He's on his honeymoon." And he'd wring her neck if she bothered him.

"Oh. Okay. We'll see what we can do. Thanks for this, Steph. You have no idea how tough this has been on Dad."

"Just get me that video, and we'll talk." She hit the End Call button on her steering wheel and sat there ruminating over the call. Kyle really had sounded afraid, and then grateful. The gravity of what she may have done made her stomach churn. If his dad was innocent, she'd just ruined his life, making her no better than Kyle had been ten years ago.

"She wants us to ask the police if they'll affirm his innocence. On video." Kyle pocketed his phone while watching his dad trudge toward the house, his head down, ignorant of the cold front that had swooped in. He moved as if he were lugging a car behind him. To bear that kind of burden, to be accused of something so heinous, was too heavy for any man to haul.

Kyle heard the door close on the house behind him. Good. Dad didn't need to be out here seeing those awful words.

"Makes you want to punch something, doesn't it?" Ice clouds came from Pastor Mitch's mouth as he stood there, arms crossed, fists clenched, and jaw tight.

Kyle had never seen the man so upset. "Not something, but someone."

"True."

At least Kyle had managed to be polite with Trip, though all he really wanted to do was wring her neck. How could she believe his father was capable of doing something so awful?

"I'm asking God to help me understand, to observe this situation from her point of view, but all I see is her trying to get back at me, ruining my dad's reputation in the process."

"Sometimes, we never do understand."

"That's helpful." Not.

"It's the best I've got. Sometimes we have to keep on loving someone even when it makes no sense."

"By loving, you mean not hating." He cuffed his hands together and blew into them trying to warm them. He was well aware of the verse that said love your enemies. Until now, he hadn't realized how difficult that would be.

"Actually, I'm thinking more of some verses in Matthew: reconcile with your brother, turn the other check, treat others as you want to be treated."

"The golden rule. That came from the Bible?"

"Matthew 7:12."

Interesting. The difficulty was in applying the rule.

He checked his watch and frowned as he hugged his chilled body. How long did it take police to drive a few miles? It seemed forever since he'd called about the graffiti. He just wanted to paint over it before passersby saw it and believed it, but the police had told him to leave it alone until they got there. The longer they took to arrive, the more people would see the condemning words. If the waitress at the diner was any indication, people would drool over spreading the salacious rumor, in spite of peoples' lack of knowledge of the truth.

He paced his driveway to warm himself, cognizant of the light snowflakes that chose to fall right now. Snow in May. Crazy. The world was upside down. All this made him wonder what God was trying to teach him now. It seemed every trial he'd faced since returning to his faith roots had a lesson in it. Why did learning have to hurt so bad?

A block away, a car turned onto the street. Finally, the police. The vehicle pulled tight to the curb and two uniformed officers got out. Neither looked familiar from the other day. Would they stick up for Dad in a video?

"You the owner of the home?" Officer Nelson flashed his badge at both men.

"That would be my dad, Raymond Stevens. He went inside. I'll go get him."

"Appreciate it."

Leaving Pastor Mitch to deal with the officers, Kyle hurried inside and found his dad slumped in his recliner. No TV on. No radio. Just silence that had to be pummeling the awful painted words into his mind. "The police are here." He kept his tone low.

Dad peered up but didn't move.

"They want to talk with you."

"Of course." Dad attempted standing, but fell back.

Kyle thought about offering a hand but knew Dad would push it away.

He tried standing once again, this time by sitting forward, getting his feet underneath him as he pushed up on the chair arms. It clearly wasn't easy, but he finally managed to stand. This horrendous event must have aged him a full ten years.

"I've got your back, Dad." He held out his arm for Dad to take it.

But he ignored it and plodded toward the door, without a jacket.

Kyle grabbed three from the closet. One for Dad, Mitch, and himself. Dad grunted, but put on the jacket then led the way outside.

The officers were taking pictures, checking out the graffiti, combing through the bushes below, chatting with Pastor Mitch. Kyle couldn't think of anyone better to break the ice between parties.

Kyle handed a winter coat to the pastor then put on his high school letter jacket that strained over his shoulders. He'd been a skinny thing in high school, not built for sports, but his jacket was covered with letters from music. He'd always thought Dad hadn't been proud of his musical accomplishments. If so, why would he have kept the jacket?

"Mr. Stevens." Officer Nelson broke through Kyle's musing, his pen poised over a notepad.

Then Kyle realized the Mr. Stevens he was talking to was his Dad.

"Did you see who did this?"

Dad shook his head.

"Tell me about your morning." The officer wrote and spoke simultaneously.

"Kyle and I had breakfast, and after my son left for work, I showered, and then—"

"The graffiti wasn't there when you left?" Officer Nelson glanced at his notes. "Kyle, is it?"

"Yeah, Kyle Stevens." He stuffed his hands deep into his pockets. "I left right after breakfast. Pulled out of my garage." He nodded to the right of his dad's unit. His had been spared. "I backed out, so I would have seen it if it was there."

"And what time did you leave?"

"Around seven forty-five. Got to church a little before eight, I think." He looked to Pastor Mitch for confirmation, and his friend nodded.

"Mr. Stevens." The officer turned his attention back at Dad. "What were you doing when you first became aware of the message?"

Dad mimicked Kyle's hands-in-the-pocket stance. "I like to take a walk after lunch. Today it was one-ish, I think." He looked to Kyle for clarification.

"I can check what time you called." Kyle dug out his phone, brought up the call log, and nodded. "One-oh-five." At least that gave them a somewhat narrow time frame to look at. The act would have been done during daylight so, chances were, someone saw them.

"We're gonna take a walk, see if your neighbors are cooperative."

Kyle hoped people would speak up to right a terrible wrong.

The officers went to canvas the neighborhood, and all three men went inside the townhome. Pastor Mitch had promised to stick around until after the police left. Neither Kyle nor his dad argued. He found store-bought cookies in Dad's cookie jar and plated them, then poured three cups of coffee to warm their bones.

He sat in his mom's favorite chair, a glider rocker she'd

had for as long as he could remember. Sitting there made him miss her all the more. What he'd give to have more time with her, moments he'd been too self-absorbed to care about. If only the people in his old church had called him on his behavior. But they—congregation and staff—had been too cowardly to bring attention to a wrongdoing, or they were afraid to be labeled as judgmental.

Wait.

What about Trip?

Groaning, he slumped in the rocker. Hadn't this mess been created because she *had* spoken up about what she perceived as a wrongdoing? Earlier he'd asked God for perspective. Nothing like it landing in his lap with a thud.

"Problem?" Pastor Mitch leaned toward him from the couch, keeping his voice low.

Kyle smirked while glancing at his father snoring lightly in his recliner. "Isn't there always?"

"True. And I always listen."

Also true. "I just realized I'm a hypocrite."

A knock sounded on the door.

Kyle leaped up to get it, realizing he really didn't want to get into that deep of a conversation, especially now, especially in front of his father.

The two officers stood there.

Officer Nelson did the speaking, as usual. "Neighbors didn't see anything, but we'll keep looking. Go ahead and paint. We'll keep you apprised of our progress."

"We appreciate it."

The officers strode to the car, their heads on a constant

swivel.

Shoot, he hadn't gotten a video of them exonerating his dad.

"One second," he called out. Stocking-footed, he jogged toward the officers. "We have a favor to ask of you both."

They eyed him as if he were the guilty one. He sure wouldn't want to face either in an interrogation.

He gulped and forced out the words. "Um, the accuser put out a vlog showing Dad at the park, and it's gone viral."

They both nodded.

"We're aware." Finally, the other officer spoke.

"It's because of the video that this happened." He gestured toward the house. "The vlogger doesn't believe Dad's innocent, but said she'd believe you. Is it possible for me to film you guys explaining that Dad's not guilty? Then we can stop the spread."

"Better yet." Officer Nelson again. "We'll contact the local news station, see if they'll do a story, if your father wouldn't mind."

"I think he'd do anything to clear his name."

"We'll be in touch." Officer Nelson tipped his cap and got in on the passenger side.

Kyle resisted doing a little dance. Finally, the world would see that his dad was innocent, and if the news broadcast the video, the truth should reach the entire city and Dad could stop worrying.

He hurried back into the house and shared the news. For the first time since Kyle and Pastor Mitch arrived home, his dad looked relaxed. He even closed his eyes. Seconds later, he was snoring.

All their problems were far from solved, but at least this was a step in the right direction.

"Now, what were we talking about?" No surprise, Pastor Mitch hadn't forgotten their previous conversation.

Kyle had no desire to get into that anymore, so he shrugged. "I don't remember."

"Hmm, something about you being a hypocrite."

"Aren't we all?" Kyle forced a grin.

"You're deflecting."

"You're turning counselor on me."

"Sorry. Comes with the job." Pastor shrugged. "But I do think you were onto something important, something you want to get out. You were talking about wanting the police to find a witness, someone who would speak out against a wrong."

Any positive feelings Kyle had had about the police talking with the news vanished. Pastor Mitch was right, naturally. Kyle was a hypocrite. He spoke quietly, hoping not to disturb his father, "The thing is, I'm upset at Steph for speaking out when she witnessed what she felt was a dangerous situation, but then I'm also angry with church leaders who didn't confront me when I was ignoring the Bible. Is there a middle ground? Or is that being too wishy-washy?"

"Tough theological question. I even like the term wishy-washy." Pastor grinned. "It's true, we're instructed not to be double-minded or lukewarm. We're even advised to approach fellow believers when one is doing something wrong."

"That's what I thought. So, why did True North not condemn me for living with Ronnie? Shouldn't their leaders, or at least the pastor—her dad specifically—have approached me? Their acceptance of my behavior told me that I wasn't doing anything wrong. Their acceptance hurt me, Ronnie, and mostly my daughter."

"Well, I can't speak for your former church—"

"I can't either." Dad butted in, startling Kyle. Guess he wasn't asleep. "But I can speak for your mom and me. *We* raised you to do the right thing. You heard from us all along that we didn't approve of your shacking up with Ronnie, especially as a music minister in that church, but all that mattered to you was your church's approval. Why didn't the lessons from your mom and me make a difference? If they had, none of us would be in this predicament right now."

Kyle sat back in the chair, struck dumb with the truth. His parents had raised him with good morals. It wasn't until his mistake with Trip that his faith took a dive. It was all him.

To think he'd been blaming the church for his behavior when he had no one to blame but himself. If he had followed his parents' teaching ten years ago, he wouldn't have hurt Trip, and she wouldn't have the chip on her shoulder today. Kyle wouldn't have fathered a child out of wedlock, and the separation wouldn't have been so easy for Ronnie. If only he had listened to his parents, none of them would be in this predicament today.

"I see you blaming yourself, Kyle."

How did Pastor Mitch do that? "Are you clairvoyant or what?"

"Years of practice." The pastor braced his hands on his knees and again leaned toward Kyle. "We have no clue how life would have turned out if you'd made different choices in the past, so don't anchor yourself to guilt because of that. Take it all to God, lay it all at His feet. He promises forgiveness."

Kyle shook his head. "How many prodigals do you know who run from home to church? How many have to leave their church to become closer to God?"

"I don't have an answer to this, but I can assure you that you're not alone."

That didn't make Kyle feel any better, but there was something that could. He glanced at his father. "Can you forgive me?"

Dad closed his eyes and his cheeks grew taut.

Tension permeated the room, and Kyle stared down at the living room carpet. He would certainly understand if his dad didn't forgive him. This whole mess was his fault.

"Son."

Kyle jerked his head toward his father, who gave a slow nod.

"I forgive you. And I hope you can forgive me for being so obstinate and for not recognizing that your passions and God-given gifts weren't what I had planned for you."

Kyle took in a deep, cleansing breath. "Thank you," he said barely above a whisper. "And yes, I forgive you too." He forced a sad smile. "Guess we both messed up, huh?"

Dad's lips lifted slightly. "Don't know how your mother put up with us."

"She was a saint."

"That she was."

Kyle just wished it hadn't taken her dying for him and Dad to get their acts together.

Problem was, this was just the beginning of him making amends. He had to live the forgiveness he both sought and offered. And then, there were the others he'd hurt in his prodigal life as a music minister. Other Christians had hurt him as well.

He turned to Pastor Mitch, who'd sat silent during the father-son exchange. "I still hold a lot of anger toward True North. Do I have a responsibility to confront them? Or do I just say, 'I forgive you' and move on? Then what do I do about Trip? Ronnie?" And even more importantly, "What about Evie? She's the innocent one in all of this mess."

"That's a lot of questions."

"And there are plenty more where those came from." You'd think that a man who'd spent his entire adult life working in a church setting would be able to answer his own theological questions, but he'd only used the Bible to pick and choose those verses that affirmed him, and he'd made excuses for those that hadn't. He wasn't alone in that, though. Much of True North had followed that same road, all heading in the opposite direction of the real true north.

"I could make it easy for you and just point you in the right direction, but I think you need to dig into the Word. For your homework this week, start with Romans 8:1. As always, read the context around the verse."

Kyle nodded and stored that chapter and verse in his

memory as the pastor kept talking.

"And then research what you think you should do about all your questions, and we'll talk about it next week."

"A whole week?"

"I have a feeling you might need longer." Pastor Mitch winked.

And for some reason that stoked fear in Kyle because he believed reconciliation would absolutely take more than a week. It could take the rest of his life.

Steph came inside her studio apartment, hung her jacket on the coat tree, and then slumped onto her daybed that pulled double duty as couch and bed. Nights like this, when she was exhausted, that duo purpose served her well. That last rider had taken her all the way to Eau Claire, Wisconsin, a two-hour drive one way. Usually, she'd love the drive and use it to come up with new song lyrics, but the dude had talked about himself the entire ride there, employing colorful words her mother would have used soap to wash away. Thankfully, her rider back to Rochester was silent as it took her the whole drive home for her ears to recover. Oy! But the verbose passenger had tipped very well, which meant she could clock out for the evening and just veg.

And so far, not a word from Kyle. So, the police didn't want to help him after all. Not a surprise. That meant she was done with the jerk for good.

She kicked off her shoes, toed off her socks, and rested her feet on the ottoman in front of her. Now this was the life. She'd eschewed the full-time careers the rest of her family pursued. Her dad was a contractor, her mom had been a roofer, her sisters were teachers, and her younger brother a cop. That lifestyle just wasn't her. Although she did often wonder what direction her life would have gone in if she'd finished that last semester of college.

She still could if she wanted.

If she wanted. Why spoil a good thing. Being a rideshare driver gave her the freedom to do what she loved. She eyed the guitar on its stand in the corner of her living room. Without new lyrics, playing felt futile. So maybe she could binge watch that new show all her friends were clamoring about.

She flicked on the TV, and Nirvana's "Stay Away" sang from her phone. Kyle's new ringtone. This way she could mentally prepare for whatever lie he wanted to sell. "Hello." She answered generically so he wouldn't get the impression that she'd saved his number.

"Hey, Steph, this is Kyle."

She set the call to speaker and placed the phone on her ottoman. "What do you want?" Oh, she knew what he wanted, but she didn't plan to make it easy on him.

"Watch KRTV news at ten tonight."

The news? "Why?"

"Your suggestion to talk to the police was a good one. They took it a step further and contacted the news, who sat down with both Dad and the police."

So, he really was innocent?

Don't make any judgments until you watch the news.

She cleared her throat, which suddenly felt scratchy. "I'll watch." Then she swiped away his call. If Kyle's dad wasn't guilty, she had no plans to be on the phone with Kyle when the story came on so he could gloat.

She clicked over to channel 11, crossed her legs in front of herself, and cuddled a stuffed elephant to her chest. The station led with breaking news about a liquor store robbery, followed by some world event and some commercials, the weather, and finally *the* story.

Holding her breath, she watched. Two officers stood on each side of Ray. They explained that a complaint had been registered against him by a concerned citizen and that a video of the incident had gone viral, but in checking out the story, they'd learned Ray was simply honoring his deceased wife.

The story continued, but Steph heard none of it. Bile lurched up her throat, and she rushed to the bathroom, making it there just in time to lose her supper in the toilet.

She'd accused—no, not just accused, but *sentenced* an innocent man in front of the world.

She fell back on the tile floor, leaned against the wall, and hugged her knees to her chest. How could she have been so blind? So callous? What kind of person had she become that she'd almost gleefully convicted an innocent man, all in the name of being bold? That wasn't bold, it was cowardly.

She tore toilet paper from the roll and wiped her eyes, her nose. How could she make this right? She had to make it right.

There was only one person she knew who could point her in that direction: her mother. Oh, was Mom going to be disappointed in her third daughter once again. This was the kind of mistake that might never go away.

Chapter Six

Despite the late time, Steph made the hour-plus trip to her parents' home without calling first. She couldn't. Her mom would have suspected something was up and would have worried until Steph arrived. Steph couldn't do that to her. She'd hurt enough people this week with her selfish actions.

She drove up the long blacktop driveway and parked in what Dad called the Winter parking lot. Tonight, her vehicle was the only one there. The expansive and quiet yard was lit by a single light near the pole shed. At midnight, no doubt both her parents were asleep, but this couldn't wait. A man's reputation was on the line.

She grabbed her overnight bag from the hatchback and hurried to the house, her key in hand. The porch light illuminated and briefly blinded her as she climbed the porch steps, and then the front door opened.

Mom *and* Dad.

"I thought that was you." Dad opened the screen door and held it while Steph stepped inside. "What's wrong?"

She shook her head, not wanting to answer or to talk

until she was snuggled against her mom on the couch. She hung her jacket on a hook in the entry then made her way into the living room where she flicked on the fireplace. Then she grabbed the blanket from the back of the couch and curled up.

Mom must have known this was a talk for girls only, because she came into the room by herself. She sat beside Steph and wrapped the blanket around both of them. The one thing Steph hated about living alone was the lack of hugs, something her wellbeing required. Maybe that was why she'd gone off the rails with that vlog post.

Maybe that was just an excuse.

"Sweetheart, what's wrong?" Mom swiped Steph's bangs to the side.

Steph leaned into her mother's shoulder and closed her eyes. "I messed up big time, Mom, and I don't know how to fix it."

"Want to tell me about it?"

Steph shook her head because the truth was, she didn't want to tell anyone. But this wasn't about what she wanted anymore, this was about making things right.

"I hurt someone, badly, with my vlog. I shared something I thought was true and it went viral, but it wasn't what I thought. And now I've ruined a man's life." She hiccupped a sob. Her mom always thought she was overly dramatic. In this case, she wasn't.

Mom stroked her hair, running her fingers through the curls that so easily tangled, just as a lie tangled people's lives. "I saw the news tonight. I thought you might want to talk."

Steph groaned. "So, you know what a complete and utter failure I am."

"What I know is that you are a passionate young woman who's always looked out for the underdog."

Steph leaned back and peered in her mother's eyes. "Do you know who that underdog is?"

Mom shook her head. "He appeared to be familiar, but I couldn't place from where."

"Remember that worship minister I dated about ten years ago?"

Mom's face pinched. "I do."

The last time Steph had come home crying was after the fallout from her relationship with Kyle. Clearly a mother never forgets who hurts her baby chicks.

"It was his dad, Kyle's dad, and the man was innocent."

"Oh baby, I'm so sorry." Mom drew Steph close.

Steph sniffled. "All he was doing was watching a video of him and his deceased wife singing. So not only did I chase the police after an innocent man, I did it when he was grieving. I'm despicable."

"Shhh." Mom whispered into Steph's hair. "You are not despicable. You made a mistake—we all make mistakes."

"Yeah, but this is a very public mistake. A very public accusation. There's no way I can stuff that genie back into the bottle."

"Isn't there?"

"How?" She sat up and wiped her arm across her eyes. "My vlog went viral. That meant thousands of people watched that video. Thousands of people now believe Kyle's dad is a pervert."

"That may be true, so what are you going to do about it?"

"I don't know."

"You don't?"

"That's why I came here. You always have the answers."

"Hmm." Mom kissed her forehead. "I think you're old enough to come up with your own answers."

"But—"

Mom placed a finger over Steph's lips. "On top of being passionate, you're an intelligent young woman. Sleep on it. Pray about it—"

"As if God'll listen to me."

"He always does, sweetheart. Bring the problem to Him. Think about what is in your power to do. I've no doubt that, if you take this to God, He'll work right alongside you."

"You're not helping." Sighing, Steph wiped a hand over her hair.

"Okay, how about this, then." Mom pulled away then picked up her Bible from the end table. For as long as Steph could remember, the worn, dog-eared Bible had sat there. Frequently, she had found her mom seated on the couch, the Bible open on her lap. Mom was either reading or praying or making notes in the margins. Whether or not Steph agreed with what was in between the covers, that book was a precious treasure.

Oh, to have a faith like that.

"I want you to have this." Mom handed over the Bible.

But Steph pushed it away. "It's yours. You love this book."

"Yes, I do, and I can get another one."

"But—"

"God's Word isn't something we keep to ourselves, sweetheart. This book has been meant for you since you were born, and I've held on to it far too long. But I do have a challenge for you."

Naturally.

"Think about the times in your life when you've really been hurt, like when you didn't make Jazz Choir, or when Kyle broke up with you. What was your response then? Would you do it the same now? If not, what can you learn about your response?"

Sounded reasonable. "I can do that." She accepted the treasure and held it close to her chest. But what did Mom's questions have to do with this Bible?

"Good. Now I'm heading back to bed. Your sister's bringing her girls over tomorrow, and I need my rest to keep up with them."

"Thanks, Mom."

"You're welcome, sweetheart." She patted her daughter's knee. "I'll leave you with one verse to look up. It's one that's likely saved our marriage more than once."

Steph felt her eyes bug out. She couldn't imagine her parents ever having any marital trouble.

"James one nineteen. A lot of wisdom packed into those few words." Mom leaned over and pressed a kiss to Steph's forehead. "I'll see you for breakfast tomorrow, assuming you get up that early."

"Oh, I wouldn't miss your breakfast for anything."

Would sure beat the healthy but not-exactly-tasty breakfast drinks she usually blended.

Steph followed her mom upstairs and veered off to her old bedroom that had now become a nursery.

Sadness weighed heavy on her shoulders as she stared at the empty crib. Mom was right about two of Steph's biggest life hurts, but no one knew about the third. Asking to use Carrie's or Ginny's old rooms would prompt questions she wasn't certain she ever wanted to answer. Instead, she sat on her bed, now populated with stuffed animals, and propped open Mom's Bible. Not that she intended to read it, but seeing Mom's wise scribblings in the borders gave her peace.

Now what was it Mom wanted her to consider? Her immediate response to life's hurts, that was it.

Not making the jazz choir her senior year of high school had been a huge blow. In the past, all seniors had made it in. Steph had invited a new girl in their school to try out, an outgoing junior with an amazing voice.

Naturally, the new girl had made it in, bumping off Steph, the quiet kid who wouldn't make waves. Like a good girl, she'd stepped back, congratulated the new girl.

No. Change that. She hadn't stepped back, but pulled away. Shut down, so she couldn't be hurt again.

She hadn't been hurt like that again until Kyle. But the real pain from him came long before the breakup, which had occurred because she'd once again shut down.

Then losing the baby had devastated her.

She cradled her hands over the stomach that had once

carried a nine-week-old child no one but she and her doctor had known about. She'd shut down even more after the miscarriage. Hadn't finished her last semester of college. Had closed her Bible for good. Then she'd found the studio apartment in Northfield where she could feel sorry for herself under the guise of wanting to be independent. Of wanting to spend time writing music instead of working a career job like her successful, confident siblings.

With this new setback, would she behave the same way? Shutting down would certainly be the least painful. She could easily forget vlogging and spend her life driving, but getting nowhere.

Couldn't she?

She looked down at the Bible in her lap and began paging through it. What verse had Mom recommended? James, wasn't it? Yes, James one something.

She flipped toward the end of the Bible until she found James and read the first chapter, all soundbites of wisdom, until she reached verse nineteen.

> *"Know this, my beloved brothers:*
> *let every person be quick to hear,*
> *slow to speak, slow to anger..."*

Whoa. Having grown up reading the Bible, the verse wasn't unfamiliar to her, but now it took on a whole new meaning. She could see how those words would be wise not only for married couples, but for all people.

Especially popular vloggers.

She hadn't listened, but instead ran at the mouth in anger over a perceived wrong. If only she would have listened and done some research before she spoke, no one would have been hurt.

Just thinking about that wore her out. She could sleep forever.

Wasn't there a verse about going to God and Him giving us rest? More than anything, that was what she needed because life was just too hard.

Looking for a single verse among the thousand-some pages in this book was also too hard, but she had a solution for that. She took out her phone and did a google search. There it was, Matthew 11:28 – 30. She returned to her mom's Bible and paged to the first book of the New Testament. No surprise, Mom had it underlined:

"Come to me, all who labor and are heavy laden,
and I will give you rest."

Beside the verse, Mom had written: *Praying Stephenie will find the Rest she's seeking.*

"I want that too, Mom, I do," she whispered. "But when Kyle hurt me, I..."

Was it really Kyle's fault?

Where had that thought come from? Of course, it had been Kyle's fault. He was the music minister. He should have known better than to have sex with her.

And you didn't?

"I..." She looked upward, her finger raised to make a

point, but excuses failed her. She closed the Bible, not liking the conviction coming from it, but that didn't stop her conscience from eating at her.

Truth was, she was just as much to blame as Kyle had been, and that was what really bugged her.

Her choices weren't God's fault. Rather, she'd shut Him out because of her shame, then once she'd shut Him out, she hadn't had to worry about shame anymore. Or so she thought. Every poor choice she'd made since then still dogged her, and here she tried to justify her actions on her vlog as being bold and strong.

Add "stupid" to that.

Which was what spreading that rumor about Kyle's dad had been.

Once again, she opened the Bible. It had to have something to say about spreading rumors. Wasn't there a *VeggieTales* show about a *Rumor Weed*? Apparently, she hadn't watched it enough. She went to her phone again and asked what the Bible said about spreading rumors.

Pages of verses came up, but two stood out. Exodus 23:1 warned about spreading false reports, and Ephesians 4:29 exhorted people to only speak of what's helpful in building up others, not tearing them down.

Was that what she'd done with Kyle's dad? Yes, she'd believed he had done something wrong, and reporting it to the police had been the right thing to do. But—and this was a big but—telling the entire world about his actions before she had the facts had been very wrong. She'd essentially opened up Pandora's box. Not even taking the video offline and issuing an apology, as she would do later this morning, would undo her actions.

And that made her want to throw up again.

Instead, she looked toward her ceiling, searching, hoping God was listening. It had been years since she'd talked to Him.

"I messed up big time, God, and I don't know what to do next. I know it's been a long time since I've asked for Your guidance, and my life shows it, but I'm asking again. A billboard spelling out Your answer would be nice, by the way. Thanks."

Hopefully, God had a sense of humor.

Regardless, she closed Mom's Bible and laid down in her former bed surrounded by her nieces' stuffed animals.

Even in the midst of the biggest storm she'd experienced in years, she actually felt at peace.

Kyle sat upright on his bed, his new Bible open on his lap. Too many thoughts and questions swirled through his brain for him to get any sleep. Had Trip watched the newscast? If so, would she agree to vlog her apology? Would that make any difference, or was it too little too late to restore his dad's reputation.

He just had to remember Romans 8:1. "There is therefore now no condemnation for those who are in Christ Jesus." No condemnation. None. For all he'd done wrong.

In Jesus, he was free. That entire chapter of Romans affirmed that nothing could separate him from Jesus. Wow. How had he not seen that before?

Wrapping his head and heart around the truth could take a while.

Then there were all the questions he'd bombarded Pastor Mitch with. One thing he'd confirmed through his reading and research was that he needed to apologize to those he'd hurt. That apology not only had to be sincere, but he had to live it out. That would be the challenge, especially when it came to Ronnie. As for his old church, he'd research what to do with them another time. As Pastor Mitch had warned, this could be a long process.

For now, Kyle retrieved a notebook from his living room and began to make a list of those with whom he needed to pray about and make amends. At the top of the page he wrote *Pray for*. Then he made a list of names.

Dad

He put a checkmark by that one. Not that it was a one and done, but they were on the road to healing.

Trip

Perhaps he should make an effort to call her by her real name, not the endearment he'd given her shortly after they'd met. No doubt, she now had an aversion to the nickname.

Ronnie

The difficulty with her was wanting to place half the blame on her. But he alone was responsible for his actions. He hadn't treated her as he should have, even though he had followed her lead. After all, she was the pastor's daughter. He'd convinced himself that she wouldn't behave in a way that was contrary to God's teaching. Crazy how once he'd allowed the devil to have a foothold in his life, it had been easy to keep heading down the wrong path, all the while convincing himself he wasn't doing anything wrong.

That meant he should also add her parents to the list, regardless of the fact that they'd accepted Kyle's role in their daughter's life.

Pastor Dean and Cheryl Whitmer

Now that Kyle had a daughter of his own, he had an entirely new perspective on his own behavior.

Evie

Writing his daughter's name broke his heart more than anything. Because of him, she'd grow up only knowing a broken family. How do you begin to reconcile that?

True North

And how do you go about apologizing to an entire

congregation? Would Pastor Dean give him the pulpit for a few minutes? They'd always gotten along, and he'd been upset when Ronnie had broken up with Kyle, but Kyle hadn't spoken to the man since shortly after the breakup, when Kyle had moved on to New Hope.

And then there was the other tougher subject he needed to pray about: confronting True North. Was that the right word? Probably not, but that was what came to his mind right now. As with any of the above, he needed to do a lot of praying and digging into the Word before he took any actions.

His heart heavy, Kyle set down his notebook and pen and leaned back in his recliner. Pastor Mitch would caution him against getting down on himself so much. He was forgiven! And that meant writing down some blessings, too.

He retrieved his paper and pen and turned the page. At the top he wrote *Blessings*. The first one was easy.

Evie

How something so beautiful could come out of disobedience, he'd never understand. All he could do was give thanks and be obedient in his fatherhood.

Speaking of fatherhood...

Kyle wrote...

Dad

It took his mom's death for him to start reconnecting

with his father. Why had it taken a tragedy to bring them back together? So much wasted time. But the blessing was, they were reconciling, and they were establishing a relationship Kyle had never dreamed possible. He would do whatever he could to nurture that relationship.

New Hope

Their job offer had come at the perfect time. Ronnie had simultaneously announced her pregnancy and that she was leaving him for someone else. She'd insisted there was no chance the baby was the new boyfriend's. Following that double whammy, he needed a place to escape to where he wouldn't see her with the new boyfriend. Why they'd offered a poser like him a job, he didn't know. Someday he'd ask Pastor Mitch, but for now he'd be grateful he'd gotten the job in a church that worshipped God and not big attendance numbers.

Speaking of Pastor Mitch, now *there* was a blessing. Kyle wrote down his name while grinning.

Pastor Mitch

Before Pastor Mitch, no one had confronted Kyle about his life choices. Yet somehow the pastor had done it with love and kindness. He really had spoken the truth in love. Apparently, Kyle had hungered for it, because it wasn't long before God tore the veil from his eyes.

Kyle yawned and blinked. At last he was getting tired. He

certainly had more blessings than the ones he'd written down, but it was a good start. He brought the notebook back to his bedroom and prayed over each name until he fell asleep.

His cell phone playing an annoying tune jolted him awake. The notebook slid to the floor with a *whomp* as he reached for the phone to check who was calling before the sun had barely risen.

Trip?

He fumbled, swiping the Answer button a couple times before succeeding. "Tri...Stephenie?"

"I watched the news last night."

And? Not wanting to fill in the blanks incorrectly, he remained silent, waiting for her to expound.

"And I'm sorry." The words whispered across the phone line.

Warmth coursed through his body at her words, and he answered with the same difficulty she'd shown in apologizing. "Thank you."

"I'll be recording and posting my apology this morning."

He sat up in the bed, now fully awake. "Dad will appreciate that."

"But I do have one request from you now."

"Sure. Name it."

"I'd like to get together. Talk."

Whoo boy. That was on his to do list as well, but it still made him nervous. "That's a good idea. You name the time and place, and I'll be there." Hopefully, Pastor Mitch would grant him time off if needed.

"Would you mind meeting at my place? I think what we need to talk about requires privacy."

"I agree. Your place is fine."

"Good. How about tomorrow, say noon-ish?"

"I'll be there." She lived close enough to his church. He could take his lunch hour then. "See you tomorr—"

"Wouldn't you like my address?"

"I remember where I dropped you off."

She laughed softly. "Well, that wasn't exactly where I lived. I didn't want you to know my address."

"Oh."

He wrote down her correct address before disconnecting, then he just stared at his phone wishing he could call back and cancel. He had a feeling about what she was going to tell him, and knew he wasn't going to like it. That just meant he had to don God's armor to prepare.

Steph clutched her phone, staring down at it. Words failed her. She was about to confess to the whole world that she'd messed up big time, when all she wanted to do was run and hide from that world.

But that would be cowardly, and she was done being spineless.

One thing her mom had reminded her about was that she didn't traverse this path alone, so she set down her phone, looked upward, and asked for words.

For today and for tomorrow. Both filled her with anxiety. Confessing could end her vlogging career for good. Meeting with Kyle could challenge all she'd come to believe over the past years, and that wouldn't make her bold and sassy, it would make her a fool.

Chapter Seven

Steph held her breath as she brought up her apology vlog post the next morning. The number of views were nowhere near that of the viral post, and most likely never would be. Too many around the world would see Kyle's dad as a vile man and never learn of his innocence, and that broke her heart.

She glanced at the comments and cringed. Usually, her posts preached to the choir and the comments were filled with atta girls, but not today. She should turn off the computer, prepare some kind of food for when Kyle arrived, but she was drawn to the comments as if they were a chocolate-covered donut. There were a lot of "How could you?" condemnations. A handful of readers appreciated her honesty. Pretty much everyone was an expert on the topic, and very few showed restraint in voicing their opinion. Too many laced those opinions with obscenities.

When had humanity gone from preaching tolerance, to a world filled with finger-wagging judgment? Social media had given everyone a pulpit from which to preach, herself included, but few had the degree or experience that gave credence to the sermon.

If she'd learned anything from this incident, it was that her words carried weight, so she had a responsibility to investigate before reacting. Just a smidgen of research would have proven Ray's innocence. That made her wonder what else she may have gotten wrong since the beginning of her vlog. Starting tomorrow, she planned to go through each post to verify the truth, and where she'd gone wrong, she would publish the truth.

She closed her laptop, crossed her arms over the top, and laid her head on her arms. Already she was weary just thinking of the monstrous task in front of her. Including lunch with Kyle.

But she wouldn't accomplish anything by sitting and feeling sorry for herself. She got up and pulled sandwich meat, tomatoes, lettuce, and condiments from the fridge. Before Kyle broke up with her, he'd bragged about going vegan. If he didn't like what she put out, that wasn't her problem. Back when she'd dated him, she would have gone grocery shopping just for him.

Not anymore. She no longer needed to win his favor—that was one way she'd grown bold in the years since the breakup.

Being bold also meant acknowledging your mistakes, making amends, and moving forward. She internalized the acronym, Triple A—Acknowledge * Amend * Act—so she could add it to her website. In the future, she would not post without adhering to another acronym, the 3R's: Regard * Research * React.

Going forward, prayer would inform each step. It had to. Without it, she created huge messes.

Her next vlog would be on those Triple A's and 3R's. If others could learn from her mistakes, that would make this entire event a whole lot easier to live with.

She arranged food on her rolling island then set her two-person table. She'd always loved the intimacy of this studio apartment, but the mere thought of being alone in here with Kyle gave her claustrophobia. Going someplace public wouldn't do, though. With what she had to tell him, she had a feeling there could be heated words, but he needed to hear what she should have told him years ago.

With fifteen minutes until he arrived, if he got there on time, she primped a bit too much in the mirror. Ten years ago, she'd been a good twenty pounds heavier. Her hair had been too long, but it had done a good job of hiding her face. That insecure girl had been banished, but Steph still felt the need to look her best when Kyle arrived.

Barefooted, she stepped out of the bathroom just as a knock sounded on the door. She glanced at her watch. Huh, three minutes early. That would be a change.

She took her time going across the small apartment, not wanting to give the impression that she was excited to see him. She peeked through the eye hole. Yep, it was Kyle. A new Kyle. It was as if they'd traded places fashion-wise. He'd once been all about styling himself like your typical worship leader, but now, he wore regular jeans and a button-down shirt. His hair didn't look highlighted or gelled at all.

Whereas, she'd become more interested in style, cognizant of how confident it made her feel. The look wasn't for others as much as it was for herself.

He knocked again, and she finally opened the door.

His eyes widened. Still surprised by her change? That didn't hurt her ego either.

"Come on in." She motioned to the table, where they would sit across from each other. No way was he sitting on her daybed. "Thanks for coming."

"Thanks for asking." He removed his shoes and left them by the door, then handed her a paper bag. "Still like chocolate old-fashioneds?"

"Really?" She glanced in the bag. A chocolate and a glazed donut. "Still my favorite, but it's not vegan, is it?"

"You're vegan now?"

She snorted. Really? "Nope." And he didn't need any more explanation than that. "What about you?"

"Gave it up a year ago." He shrugged. "Decided life wasn't worth giving up hamburgers for, but mostly I decided that I was tired of living to impress people."

Hmm. That would explain the outfit and the hair. Not that he still didn't look good, but before, he'd always appeared to be trying too hard. Well, that had been her opinion *after* their breakup.

"Have a seat." She gestured again to the table. "I know you're on break, so I don't want to waste your time." She sat, then realized she'd forgotten a beverage. "Want something to drink? I've got sparkling waters. Some raspberry-blackberry or strawberry-mango."

"Strawberry-mango sounds good."

She brought him a can then sat at the table.

"Mind if I say grace?" He folded his hands.

"Be my guest." This should be interesting. He used to love hearing himself pray aloud, at least that was the impression he'd given.

"Father, thank You for this time You've given us. I pray You'll give me a listening ear and that Stephenie will not fear telling the truth. Open both our hearts and eyes to You. And thank You for this lunch she's prepared. And have I said how grateful I am that I can eat meat?"

She chuckled at that.

"Please bless this food to our bodies, and bless our time together. In Jesus' name, Amen."

She echoed the "amen" then opened her eyes and stared at him. "You've brought your prayers down a few notches."

"Right?" He shook his head. "There's a verse in the Bible that talks about praying to be heard, to gain attention. Described me to a T."

Yes, it had. She grabbed the bread off the island, diverting the subject. After plating a couple slices, she handed it to Kyle, all while formulating her words.

"There are things I need to tell you."

"And I'm here to listen." He added butter, ham, and cheese to his sandwich—definitely not a vegan anymore—along with the tomato and lettuce.

Her sandwich looked eerily similar, but her appetite vanished and that scared girl from years ago tried to squirm her way back to the front. Steph pushed her to the rear.

"I posted the apology and retraction yesterday."

"Dad and I watched it. Thank you."

"But that doesn't mean everyone who saw the first video will see this one." Blinking, she looked to the ceiling. "And I deeply regret that."

He winced but said, "You did what you could do, and we appreciate that. We have to trust God for the rest."

Now that sounded like the old, super-righteous Kyle.

She took a bite of her sandwich, but couldn't resist asking the question, "Do you really mean that?"

He shook his head and looked sincerely confused. "I don't know what you're asking?"

"What you said about trusting God. Do you mean it, or is that just something you're telling me to prove how spiritual you are?"

A sad smile curved his lips slightly upward, but she read regret in his eyes. "I was that bad." Not a question, but an understanding.

"I didn't realize it until after we broke up. It took that to see how fake you were."

"I'm sorry. I wasn't always that way, it all just..." He picked up his sandwich and grasped it tightly, stamping his fingerprints into the bread. "The attention went to my head. I have no excuse."

No, he certainly didn't. She took a bite of her sandwich and chewed it slowly, preparing for the other reason she'd wanted to see him in person.

She drank down half her can of water before gaining the courage to say the rest. "You hurt me."

He set down his now-mutilated sandwich and stared at it. "I know, and I'm sorry."

"The thing is you don't know the whole truth. I cared for you too much. And I sacrificed myself for you." She jabbed a finger to her chest. "It went against everything I'd been taught, believed, wanted for myself. All it took was that one night we had sex, and I couldn't live with my guilt. Then instead of listening or trying to understand, you broke up with me."

She stopped to wipe her nose, but refused to let tears fall.

He just kept staring down at his mangled sandwich.

Which made her feel guilty because she wasn't without blame. "But I also want you to know, that wasn't entirely your fault. I wasn't strong or confident enough to believe that you'd love me if I said 'no.' We were both playing with fire, and we both got burned. I'm deeply sorry for that."

He looked up, his eyes narrowed in confusion, but still remained silent. He must have read James 1:19 like she had, because he had the "listening" part down to a T.

"The big problem is what happened later." Now the tears really wanted to fall. The words had never left her lips before out of the fear that she'd never stop crying.

She said a quick prayer that God would give her the right words. Not condemning words, just the truth.

"You see, it turned out that one night together got me pregnant."

His jaw dropped. "What?" came out in a guttural expression. An array of emotions crossed his face from confusion to anger to sadness. "You never told me."

She wiped now-sweaty palms on her jeans and swallowed the knot that clotted her throat. "It's not that I didn't want to, but I only found out after you broke up with me. Once I took the pregnancy test, I came to your place to tell you but..." The clot in her throat grew bigger and wouldn't allow her to speak.

"You saw me with Ronnie." His tone was low and filled with remorse.

She nodded. Through the window of his apartment, she'd seen him lip locked with the pastor's daughter.

"I have no words." He shook his head back and forth, back and forth, back and forth before speaking, his voice hoarse. "And the baby?" He glanced around her apartment. Looking for evidence of a child perhaps?

She pinched her eyes closed, but still felt wetness leak from beneath her lashes. "I miscarried shortly thereafter. No one ever knew. Not even Mom." She peered up and saw tears trickling down his cheeks.

"I'm so sorry, Stephenie. You never should have had to deal with that alone. I have no words for my behavior then, other than that I was a self-absorbed jerk."

She wouldn't argue with that because it was the truth. "Still, I should have told you, and I'm sorry I didn't. I turned my back on God after that, but He's grabbing my attention again." Why did it always take big mistakes for someone to realize they needed God?

"I'm glad to hear that. He's got both of our attention."

Did he really mean that? Didn't matter. This next part was her responsibility, and Kyle's response was his alone to deal with. "I learned something from reading the book of Matthew a few nights ago. If I want to draw closer to God, then I need to reconcile with those who hold something against me before I can offer anything to God. Matthew also said that I need to tell the truth, but not to my vlog audience. Only to the person who hurt me. Crazy how it's much easier to tell the world than the individual."

She wiped her nose and eyes. "So, that's another reason why I invited you here today. I'm looking to reconcile. That doesn't mean we'll be friends or anything, but I'm tired of holding a grudge against you. I'm tired of blaming you when I wasn't innocent. I'm ready to start with a clean slate with God."

Suffocating silence filled her small room.

He stared at his sandwich. She nibbled at hers. He got up and looked out the front window as minutes ticked off on the wall clock. There wasn't much for him to see—just a parking lot. The lack of view helped keep her costs down. He looked at his watch and grimaced. Typed something into his phone. It chirped, and he checked the answer. Stared out the window again, then his gaze scoured the room, landing on her guitar.

His eyes flicked to hers. "You still play?"

"Every day."

"Good." He walked to the guitar and ran his fingers over the strings. "Do you mind?"

She shrugged. "Go ahead." Though part of her didn't want to hear him play again. It was his skill and passion that had drawn her to him in the first place, and then blinded her to the truth of who he was.

He picked up the guitar, the Martin she'd scrimped and saved for in high school, and ran his fingers over the strings. He tweaked the tuning—his ear couldn't handle off-key—then he tried a chord.

A slight smile grew on his face and he sat down on her daybed and picked out an unfamiliar tune. A lament that made her want to tear up again. He had that way with music—he could evoke tears from the hardest of hearts.

Then he stopped. Bowed his head, and remained that way for seconds. Minutes, before peering up. "It's still an amazing instrument."

"You still know how to summon my emotions."

His lips lifted then quickly fell. He put her guitar back in its stand then rejoined her at the table. He picked up his sandwich, brought it to his lips, but still didn't eat.

All she could do was sit there hugging herself, watching. Was he angry? Remorseful? Or maybe he didn't care at all.

But that wasn't what it seemed.

Finally, he looked up at her, locked gazes so she couldn't look away. "Thank you for your gentleness. That's more than what I deserve." He shook his head. He seemed to do that a lot. "Another time, I'd like to tell you my story, but I have to get back to work."

He picked up his dismembered sandwich and wrapped it in a napkin. "One thing I've learned recently, thanks to my remarkable pastor, is the difference between grace and mercy. Grace is an undeserved gift, while mercy is *not* receiving the punishment you deserve. You have just offered me tremendous mercy, and I thank you for that. You really have become a beautiful and bold woman, Stephenie Winter."

And with those words, he said goodbye and walked out of her apartment.

So many questions rattled around her brain. Why was he renting a place from his father, and what became of Ronnie? Their baby couldn't be much more than a year old. Had they split up since then? Why did any of that even matter to Steph?

What really irked her though, was that she suddenly missed him because the selfless man he'd become was a one-eighty change from the arrogant man he'd been.

Chapter Eight

Rain coursed outside Kyle's window while he ate breakfast, but he refused to let that get him down. Stephenie's apology had seemed to do the trick of lifting his emotions. A week and a half later, they'd found no more graffiti on the house. The waitress who'd gossiped about Dad hadn't said any more about the park incident. Dad hadn't complained about any other events, so life was nearly back to normal. It was almost too easy.

Best of all, tonight Ronnie was going to drop off Evie, and he'd get to have her for two whole weeks. Working eight hours today was going to be interminable, but then the following fortnight would probably woosh by faster than a heavy-metal guitar riff.

He finished his cereal, put his bowl in the dishwasher, then got ready for work. He scanned Evie's room, made sure it would be up to Ronnie's now-higher standards. He double-checked the living area for the childproofing required with a one-year-old. As far as he could tell, the home was ready for her.

After looking in on his dad, who was in good spirits, Kyle

hurried to work. He looked forward to having lunch with Pastor Mitch today—he was ready to talk about what he'd learned from his Bible research. Unfortunately, what he'd learned showed him he needed to get in touch with Steph again. That time last week had been painful enough. He'd left her place feeling battered and bruised, yet somehow more at peace.

Problem was, he had more to say.

A bigger problem was that he'd left her place feeling some of that same old attraction. At least he'd learned—the hard way, naturally—not to make decisions based on feelings alone.

Boy was he in a ruminating mood today. He got out of his Subaru and headed into the church building. He waved to the church secretary, stopped to talk baseball with the custodian. Yeah, he was even beginning to enjoy the game, probably because it gave him and his dad a shared interest. Who'd have thunk he would not only spend time with his dad, but he'd look forward to that time.

He peeked in on Pastor Mitch and they exchanged good mornings. "See you at lunch?"

"Wouldn't miss it."

Kyle couldn't believe that he actually looked forward to digging into the Bible now. Amazing what getting out of a toxic church could do for your spiritual health.

He arrived in his office, a windowless room he spent little time in other than to do some necessary paperwork. He preferred working in the sanctuary, where light filtered through the stained-glass windows that depicted several scenes from the Bible, both Old Testament and New. True North had spent little time in the Old. That alone should have been a red flag to him.

It also bothered him that Evie was going to grow up in that "politically correct" over "Biblically correct" atmosphere. That would definitely be a challenge down the road. But today, he simply had to focus on loving her, which was not difficult at all.

He carried his guitar to the sanctuary to work on Sunday's offering hymn. He sat on the steps that led to the pulpit area and picked through the beginning, but the hymn somehow morphed into something different, the melody he couldn't erase from his mind. The song that had come to him while at Stephenie's place. Since those first picked notes, the tune had grown from lament to hope. Lyrics had come to him just as quickly, and that never happened. He wasn't a lyricist like Stephenie had been.

The words weren't quite right yet. Too "me-centered" maybe? He sang through the song again, removing the "I" references, substituting them with "we" and "us." That worked much better, but it still required tweaking.

Trip would have caught the error right away. Oh, he and Trip—Stephenie—had been a great duo back in the day, when he'd pluck out a melody and she'd pen the text. They'd even harmonized well together, with his tenor and her rich alto. If only they—*he* hadn't messed things up.

There is therefore now no condemnation
for those in Christ.

The words from Romans 8:1 filtered through his thoughts, as they often did now, reminding him he was forgiven. Those words had even found their way into this song, simply titled, "Mercy."

He played through it one more time, singing along and closing his eyes to lift the musical prayer up to God. The song closed with an acapella verse he hoped to teach the congregation someday. He sang the last word, holding onto the note in a decrescendo until silence took over.

His eyes still closed, he lifted up the prayer. *Thank You, Lord, for Your mercy.*

A single pair of hands clapping broke the silence, and other hands added to the applause.

Sheepishly, he opened his eyes and looked outward. Standing in the back of the church, the pastor, secretary, custodian, youth director, and other church staff applauded. Once upon a time, he would have eaten up the attention, but now it felt wrong to accept an ovation owed to God. So, he bowed his head and thanked God for the music and the lyrics, and prayed that they would speak to others as they'd spoken to him and to the church staff.

Moments later, he felt someone sit beside him.

Pastor Mitch, no surprise.

"Is that an original?"

Kyle shrugged. "It is."

"You're doing it on Sunday?"

"Well, not this Sunday, but soon, with the congregation coming in acapella at the end."

"Ah, they'll like that."

"Me too."

One thing he loved about this church was being able to hear the congregants sing. At True North, the band had drowned everyone out so that many just listened. How tragic that during worship, their band had stolen the focus from God.

Pastor slapped his back then stood. "Maybe at lunch you can tell me the story behind it."

"I'll think about it."

"That's all I can ask."

As the pastor made his way down the center aisle, Kyle set aside his Taylor acoustic, and his cell phone rang. Dad's tone.

Concern zipped through him as he pulled the phone from his pocket. Dad didn't call unless absolutely necessary. Kyle swiped right to answer. "Dad?"

"They're saying..." His voice trembled so Kyle could barely understand. "J...just awful things about me."

They? Who was they?

"Dad, are you home?"

A mumbled, "yes" came over the line. "And the writing is back."

Writing? Oh, the graffiti?

The tension sizzling through him gave over to burning anger. "I'll be right there." He gripped his guitar and resisted the temptation to slam it down. He looked outward, and the pastor had stopped midway to the lobby.

"Problem?"

Kyle nodded. "More graffiti and something else, I don't

know what, but Dad's shook. You don't mind—"

"Get outta here."

"Thanks." Guitar in hand, Kyle zipped out to his Subaru and broke every speed limit going home. He pulled into his driveway, and rage pulsed through him. What kind of evil being would write such despicable words? This time across the entire building? In a family neighborhood?

Kyle got out of his car and slammed the door. If Dad hadn't already called the police, that was the first thing Kyle would do. He wanted them out here now. This time the punks wouldn't get away with it. The new security system Dad had installed would have caught on camera whoever did this. He glanced up at the camera above Dad's front door and nearly repeated one of the words smeared on the house. Paint also covered the camera lens. No doubt, whoever did this had masked themselves as well so their identity would be hidden.

He knocked on his dad's door and let himself in. Dad sat in his recliner, looking like he'd aged twenty years since this morning. Kyle had no reassuring words for the man, so maybe making a plan of action would help. But first he needed information.

He sat on the couch adjacent to his dad's chair. They didn't have to look each other in the eye, which would probably make Dad even more uncomfortable answering Kyle's questions.

"Did you call the police?"

"Yep. A few minutes ago, once I got my voice back."

Good. They should be here shortly. On to the next

question. "What else happened today?"

Dad shifted in his chair, looked out the side window at the neighbor's home. "Went grocery shopping. Some woman carrying a baby came up to me, called me all sorts of names, threatened to call the police. I..." He cleared his throat. "I just left. I've shopped at that store for twenty years, and now I don't dare show my face."

Anger gripped as tight as a guitar string. Yes, Stephenie had apologized, but if not for her, his dad would be enjoying his retirement. He needed to talk to her, the sooner, the better because this had to end. Now.

"I'll talk to Steph. She's got media connections." At least, he hoped she did. "And we'll flood the town and screens with your innocence."

Dad flung out a curse word, and Kyle cringed.

"I'm not stupid, boy. Once bad news gets out of the bottle, there's no stuffing it back in. So far as I can see, there's only one solution, and that's moving."

"But—"

"Don't worry about your home. I'll rent out my unit. Maybe sell the whole kit and caboodle to you. The truth is, my name in this town is spelled M-U-D, and there's no amount of washing that'll make it clean."

"It's just not right."

"No, it's not, but unless you think of a better solution, tomorrow I start looking for a new place. Probably become a snowbird in Florida like all my friends."

Florida? Just when they were learning to like each other? There had to be another solution. And Stephenie was somehow at the heart of that solution.

Then something else occurred to him.

In just a few hours, Ronnie would be arriving with Evie. If she saw what was painted on the front of the house, she might never let him see his daughter again. In one single afternoon, he could lose both his dad and his daughter.

Chapter Nine

Tonight couldn't come soon enough. It had been well over a week since Stephenie had an evening out with Angie, and boy did she need one now. With much of the hoopla surrounding Kyle's dad having died down, she was ready to get out, even if it was just a walk and talk along the Cannon River. They could have dinner at that cute new sidewalk café and watch life return to the area on this warm spring day. They could grab some coffee a bit later and just talk. She needed time with a girlfriend because, oh, did she have stuff to tell her.

But Angie would be at school until five today, and that meant Steph had several hours to kill yet, and she didn't feel like working. She'd already gotten in several hours of driving this morning, having transported business travelers to both the Rochester and Minneapolis airports. Those were always her most lucrative trips. Dressing for success was a big part of her job, although not every passenger acted professionally.

Who was she to point fingers, though? She'd gone through a period not too long ago when she'd acted anything but professional. That was when the grapevine had told her Kyle and Ronnie were parents. After that, she'd gone through a phase of wanting to become a mom, whatever it took. She still shivered at her behavior from then and was grateful for Angie's friendship. Everyone needs that friend who is willing to speak the truth, and Angie hadn't held back. Not that Angie was exactly a saint either.

Still, Steph was certain her friend wouldn't rein herself in tonight either when Steph told her about this past week, because she was the one Steph had poured her heart out to regarding Kyle, spilling all the dirt on him. Well, all except for the pregnancy.

But the evening was hours away yet. She could go for a walk. Read a book maybe. Or...

Her gaze landed on her guitar, which she hadn't picked up since Kyle had played. She could never match his skill with the instrument, so she'd let it sit the past week, hoping his song would soon be forgotten, but the haunting tune still lingered. There was only one way to get rid of it.

From the island, she retrieved a notepad that had lyric ideas scratched on it. She sat with her guitar, trying to match music to the lyrics, but nothing came to her. If she had any guts at all she'd give Kyle a call and ask for help, but that was a door she didn't dare open. After his one visit here, it was clear her feelings toward him were still too raw.

Instead, she chorded and sang along with a familiar old song from one of her favorite artists of ten years ago, and lost herself in the prayer-filled lyrics. That song merged into another, and then another until her fingertips reminded her she hadn't played for a while, and the calluses had become soft. The music gave her a peace she hadn't experienced in months.

It was time to find a church again, worship with others again.

She set down her guitar and googled Christian churches in the area and found a smorgasbord of denominations represented. A lot of Lutheran and Catholic, naturally, Methodist, Baptist, some churches that hid their denomination behind a "hip" name. How does one go about choosing a church? Which one did Kyle work at? That one, she'd avoid.

Her phone rang Kyle's tone as she researched a church, and she just stared at the Decline button. Should she?

Nah, but she wouldn't answer either. If it were important, he'd leave a message.

Seconds after the phone quit singing, it pinged, indicating he had left a text instead of a voice mail. She opened it up and read:

– WE NEED YOUR HELP! –

A second later, a picture filled her screen, and she gasped at the words that desecrated both Kyle's and his dad's home. How could someone be so vile?

Trembling, she called him back.

He answered after one ring, and her blood chilled at the anger in his tone. "What do you plan to do about this?"

"I…" She didn't have an answer. She'd done all she knew to do. She'd taken down the video. She'd posted the apology, both in video and written form, along with the video of the police exonerating Ray. There was nothing else in her power.

In her power.

That was the answer. "Right now, I plan to come over to your house and pray."

Silence came over the line but for voices in the background, cars on the street.

Then a soft, "I'm sorry," and, "Thank you."

She got his address and hurried out to her Ford. She had no solution to this problem, but as she drove to Kyle's home, she prayed aloud that God would provide an answer. Seconds later, a thought came to her, and she pulled a quick U-turn. For this, she needed to change clothes.

As she drove toward home, she continued to pray for the next step as this first one was merely a bandage.

Finally, getting the go-ahead to cover the vandalism, Kyle drug out the cans of paint and painting supplies from his garage. He was grateful for the manual labor because it would help cool him off. What was wrong with people? Even if his dad had been guilty, two wrongs absolutely did not make a right.

He handed a roller to his dad and then poured paint into

the tray. Good thing the home was dark blue instead of white or this would take several coats to cover up the words.

The police would do what they could. The vandals had covered their faces before spraying the security camera, but prior to that, two men had been filmed. Once again, the few neighbors that were home during the time shown on the camera saw nothing. The police said it seemed like the vandals wanted to get caught as they were painting in daylight. All that mattered to Kyle was that they were caught and prosecuted.

Kyle worked alongside his dad in simmering silence, with Kyle on a ladder reaching the top boards and Dad down below. Kyle heard a vehicle pull into the driveway, but didn't dare turn to look. The last thing he needed was to fall and break some bones.

Ronnie would love that. Not.

"Got an extra brush for me?"

Steph?

He jerked his head around, and his roller hand splattered paint all over the bushes below.

"Nice job, Gracie." Dad looked up at him.

Kyle couldn't help but laugh at the blue paint streaking across his dad's face. "I like your new look." He climbed down then nodded at Steph. "We'd love someone to do the window trim."

"Just point me to a brush. I can do this in my sleep."

That she probably could. Having grown up with a contractor father, she and her siblings were skilled at home repair. He retrieved a brush from his dad's garage along with trim paint that was a few shades lighter than the siding.

"We appreciate your help." He handed over the supplies, taking note that she'd come prepared to paint dressed in holey jeans and a T-shirt that was already splattered. Even her tennis shoes had sprays of paint on them.

"If it weren't for me…" Her voice trailed off.

"Uh-uh. No condemnation, got that?"

"Sounds like a Bible verse."

"It is." The old Kyle would have shown off by spouting the entire verse and where it could be found, but here, that felt like bragging. He checked his watch and winced. Ronnie would be here with Evie in less than two hours. They needed to hurry, but he also didn't want to do a sloppy job. He owed it to Dad to do it right.

"Mind if I turn on some music?" Steph pulled out her phone.

"I'd love it." Kyle looked down and even felt like smiling for a second, watching Steph scroll through her phone, her tongue lagging out the side of her mouth just as it had years ago when she was concentrating hard.

"So long as you kids don't turn on that junk they play on the radio today."

"Who listens to the radio?" Kyle winked at Steph, waiting for a retort from his dad.

"Why mess with what works?"

Kyle grinned. "Didn't you just complain about radio music?"

"Oh, be quiet." Dad wagged a finger. "If I had extra paint,

there'd be a war going on right now."

A war. That was just what they were in the middle of, and yet, Dad was willing to make jokes. Kyle was able to smile. Steph was eager to pitch in.

"Got a glass?" Steph asked while monkeying with the volume on her phone. That was what they used to use back when they were poor kids, way back when. Music began on whatever app she was using, but being outside, the music barely traveled beyond the phone.

"I'll do you one better than a glass." He climbed down the ladder, hurried into his home, and came back out with a Bluetooth speaker and a TV tray.

"Perfect." She set up their makeshift music system, turned up the volume, and Skillet played. "How's that, Ray?"

He nodded. "Now that's music."

Kyle began singing along. He couldn't help it. When music played, he had to join in.

Paint brush in hand, Steph played some mean air guitar and rocked out on the female harmony, just like the old days. They still sounded good together.

And that broke his heart. How different would life have been if they'd just been obedient?

No condemnation...

Going forward, this was his life. And even with the trials, it was good. He was blessed. Choose joy.

Still singing along, he looked down at Steph's short and sassy hair bobbing beneath a Minnesota Twins cap. Would there be a chance she'd say *yes* to a date again? Nah, stupid idea. She'd probably throw the paint right in his face.

But...

She glanced up at him and grinned then returned back to her painting.

Maybe...

Another car pulled into the driveway, stopping all their singing.

It couldn't be. Not this early. Ronnie would never give up minutes with their daughter.

Car doors slammed as he slowly turned around, the paint dripping off his roller onto the bushes and grass.

It was Ronnie. And the fiancé. Evie remained in the Mercedes.

And fear squirmed in his gut.

"What's going on here?" Ronnie's shrill voice commanded as he climbed down the ladder, taking note that they'd barely begun to cover the horrific words.

He swallowed the donut-sized lump in his throat as he set down his roller and slowly walked toward the woman he'd shared the last ten years with, commitment free, probably because he knew a lifetime with her would never work out.

Still, it had been wrong, very wrong.

He splayed his hands, hoping to convey he wasn't responding with the same anger. "Someone vandalized Dad's home."

She just rolled her eyes, something she excelled at doing. "So, what I've heard is true." Her gaze flickered to Dad then back to Kyle.

Anger chased away his fear. "What you heard was a hideous rumor that's been squashed."

She nodded to the house. "Apparently not everyone thinks so."

"I know so." Stephenie stepped beside Kyle. "He's been exonerated."

"Wait." Ronnie stepped closer, her arms crossed. "Aren't you the one from the video? The one who filmed him in the first place?"

"I am, and I found out I was wrong."

"Interesting." Ronnie looked back at her fiancé, who hung close to the car, his arms crossed, almost looking amused by the exchange. She turned to Kyle, then Steph. And her eyes widened. "Aren't you the old girlfriend?"

"I am."

"Leave her out of this." Kyle growled and took a step toward Ronnie.

She raised her hands. "Not a problem." She turned on her high heels and strode toward the passenger side of the car, her expensive-looking dress waving in the breeze. The couple were probably heading out to some restaurant Kyle couldn't begin to afford. The fiancé just stood there in his expensive suit, silent and smirking. The jerk. What Kyle would give to smack that smirk from the guy's face.

Ronnie stopped by the passenger door and looked back. She took out her phone and snapped pictures of the house. "Our attorney will contact yours about custody."

"What?" Kyle stood frozen, trying to wrap his mind around what Ronnie had said.

"Once she sees these pictures and watches the vlog, I'm sure she won't have any trouble giving us full custody of Evie."

"You can't do that." Kyle started toward the car as Ronnie and the fiancé got in. A hand on his shoulder held him back, but Kyle shook it off and ran as the vehicle backed out of the driveway.

He only got a glimpse of Evie crying in the backseat as the Mercedes careened down the road. His hands balled into fists and he stood there, not wanting to turn back and face his father or Steph, not wanting to see the pity in their eyes.

And then they were at his sides.

Dad cuffed a hand on Kyle's shoulder. "You've got the law on your side."

"And they've got a big pocketbook on theirs."

"But you've got something even more powerful backing you up." This from Steph.

"Oh, really." He couldn't contain his sarcasm. "What would that be?"

"The power of prayer."

Steph's simple words nearly knocked him over. Some kind of Christian he was, that he hadn't once thought of praying his way through the situation. God was bigger than any of this. With Ronnie's threat to sue for full custody of their daughter, they needed to get on their knees immediately.

Be bold were the words Steph had used to psyche herself up to suggest prayer, as if she were super righteous, but the idea had entered her mind as soon as Ronnie showed up, and grew stronger with each word exchanged between the former couple. She couldn't stay quiet.

That Kyle had grasped onto the idea so quickly shocked her, though it shouldn't have, not with what she'd seen of this new man he'd become.

"We'll go to my place." Kyle strode away from the road and toward his side of the home. He held the door for both her and his father. "Have a seat."

While he went into his kitchen, she looked around the sparsely-furnished room. A card table with a couple of folding chairs. A couch. Recliner. His acoustic guitar that probably cost more than the furniture. She chose a folding chair and left the sofa to the men.

Kyle returned to the room with three bottles of water. He nodded to the couch. "That's more comfortable."

"I'm fine."

"Suit yourself." He handed her and his dad a bottle then sat on one end of the couch.

They all folded their hands, and Steph waited for Kyle to begin. When he remained silent, she looked over at him and saw that tears glistened on his cheeks. That meant prayer was up to her, a newly-returned Christian who'd always hated praying out loud. Her prayers were short and frank and ineloquent and always felt inadequate. Still, she felt nudged to take the lead and spoke from her heart, just as she always did for her vlog.

"Hey, God, I know You saw what just took place outside, and it's breaking Kyle's heart. Mine too, to be honest. Evie needs her daddy, and Kyle needs his daughter. Can you show the truth to Ronnie and her boyfriend, 'cause we're at a loss in knowing what direction to take. You're not, though. Can You show us what is the right thing to do? A billboard would be nice."

As always, her mind went blank after those few short sentences.

Then Kyle prayed, "What Stephenie said. Exactly."

"Ditto," Ray chimed in.

She kept her head down, listening to the silence, the words, "Show truth to Ronnie" on repeat in her mind like a scratched record.

Show truth.

Truth… She gulped.

That was it, and it scared her to death.

She opened her eyes and looked across at the men. Ray remained on the couch, but Kyle had gotten down on the floor, his face to the ground, his palms flat on the carpet.

It almost felt sacrilegious interrupting, but Kyle would be encouraged by her plan.

Hopefully.

She lightly cleared her throat and spoke softly to not startle the men. "I know what we have to do."

Ray looked across at her and Kyle slowly peered up, then wiped his face as he sat at the base of the couch.

"We…I have to tell the truth." Her lie had created the mess, so truth would clean it up.

Kyle shook his head. "Haven't you already done that?"

"Yes, but I need to go farther." She wiped suddenly sweaty palms on her jeans. "Our world has become so reactionary, someone has to get the word out to stop it."

"Does your vlog have that big of reach?"

"I'm talking beyond my vlog." The next part terrified her. "I'm talking about going into our schools here in town, using your situation as an example of the wrong way to use social media, showing that words are not harmless. With your blessing, of course." She looked to Ray for approval, and he nodded.

But Kyle looked skeptical. "You're talking school assemblies, right?"

"That or classroom. Whatever it takes."

"Do you really think the schools are just going to let a stranger come in and talk?"

"Well, not to brag, but my vlog does reach a lot of people, especially in this town."

He shook his head, clearly not believing.

"And I have connections. My best friend's a teacher, as are my sisters. I'm not beyond bribing all of them with donuts and ice cream."

That finally got him and Ray to laugh.

"Sure." Kyle shot her the grin that used to make her stomach go topsy-turvy. "You set it up, and I'll join you."

"You will?"

"I think hearing from both sides of the story will help, don't you?"

"Absolutely."

"And..." He stared toward the front door, but his eyes were unfocused. He gulped then puffed out a breath as if trying to blow the problem away. "I need to go back to my old church. I've got unfinished business there, apologies to make. Yeah." He nodded as if trying to convince himself that was the right thing to do. "They need to hear my story."

She'd like to know his story, too. "Can I come listen?"

Once again, he puffed out a breath. "Sure, but I want you to hear it before then."

"I think that's my cue to leave." Ray slapped his legs and stood.

"You don't have to." Kyle got off the floor and wiped his backside. "I mean, we're not going to talk right now." His gaze flicked to her. "But maybe tonight over burgers?"

Traitorous butterflies took flight in her stomach. This was Kyle, the jerkwad who'd ruined her life.

Who had now become a whole new man. She gnawed on her lower lip, trying to summon the bold and sassy woman within her. She raised her chin, and looked him directly in the eye. "As long as you realize this isn't a date."

He laughed a little too hard. "Just burgers, Trip."

"Good." She spun around, disconnecting their gaze. "It's time you guys finish your paint job. I have calls to make, talks to set up. It's time everyone knew the truth." She strode from the house without looking back because the truth was, she'd never gotten over Kyle and that utterly annoyed her.

Chapter Ten

"I t's just burgers." Kyle said to himself as he looked through his closet. Just burgers with Stephenie "Triple-E" Winter. Wasn't that how they'd began? Though burgers for that first date came from McDonald's and were shared with the cute and shy redhead from church, with three "E's" in her first name, who wrote the most amazing song lyrics.

Man, he'd had a crush on her.

He'd called her "Triple-E" to start, teasing her about how her name was spelled. As time went on, and they'd grown closer, her nickname shortened to Trip. Her cheeks used to blush to match her hair every time he'd said it, so he'd used it frequently.

He sighed with the knowing that he'd lost the right to say her pet name.

They'd been good until the night they went too far. That act had changed them both, and not for the better. Why was he so lousy with relationships?

He took out his favorite navy-blue button-down shirt. Ronnie used to say it brought out the blue in his eyes.

On second thought...

He folded the shirt and put it in the "good-bye" box filled with other clothes that reminded him too much of Ronnie. He chose the purple button-down instead, one of the new additions to his scaled-down, less-hipster wardrobe. Now he looked like a regular guy, not someone who was trying to impress.

His daughter needed, deserved to have that regular guy for a dad. Which was why "just burgers" tonight was going to be spent with Steph and her best friend and her two sisters who probably hated his guts. But as teachers, each knew how important a dad's role was.

He hoped.

He finished getting dressed and hurried out, stopping briefly to see how Dad was doing. Even if they managed to stop this rumor from spreading, Dad was considering moving to Florida. This had worn a strong man down. But once he managed to change Ronnie's mind, once Kyle had the custody he'd been awarded, then Dad seeing his granddaughter frequently would change his mind about moving. It had to.

As Kyle headed out to his car, he set the phone's GPS. Like everything in this small town, the burger place was only about ten minutes from his home.

He found the three women near the back of the restaurant. Two of them gave him scorching looks, no surprise. Steph's sisters hadn't much cared for him when he and Steph had been dating, so he could imagine what they thought of him now. The other woman gave him a once-over as if appraising him for worthiness.

"Hey," he said and pulled out the chair beside Steph, right across from the sisters, so he'd have to look at their disapproving faces all night. Yippee.

Steph gave introductions and handed him a menu. "You doing okay?"

"I guess. My blood has cooled to a slow simmer." But this wasn't about him, really. It was about informing the community that spreading rumors could, and did, ruin lives. For his dad's and Evie's sakes, he'd endure whatever glares they flung at him.

Carrie set aside her menu and looked his way. Not with a glare, really, but her lips pinched together tight enough to create a ring of wrinkles around her mouth. "Steph filled us in on what's going on. Do you have any updates?"

Ignore the scowl and answer her question. "Talked to my attorney, and we both agreed that Evie is better off up at Ronnie's place until the vandals are caught. Well, he highly suggested, and I begrudgingly agreed, as long as Ronnie knows it's temporary. If this had happened at Ronnie's place, I'd have a fit about Evie staying there, too, so I get it, but I don't have to like it."

"Just keep fighting for her. Dads are irreplaceable." Carrie picked up her menu. "What's good here?"

A cue, apparently, for him to be done talking—at least she'd affirmed him as a father—and for all of them to decide what they wanted. She had always fulfilled that firstborn role well.

He chose the Sunrise Burger, one that came with an egg

sunny-side up. Nothing vegan about that sandwich. But now they had about fifteen minutes to plan before the food came.

"So, here's what we've been discussing." Steph pushed a piece of paper in front of him. "Angie, Carrie, and Ginny are all welcoming us into their classrooms, and they said they'll film it for the rest of the school."

"You're okay with this?" He looked directly at Steph. Years ago, she'd had a terrible fear of both speaking and singing in public. Maybe with the vlog, that had changed as well.

She raised her chin, showing confidence, but her eyes said something totally different. "It was my idea."

"I will also be inviting other classrooms in," said Ginny. "Who knows, you could have a huge audience. My students have become so brash, they don't stop to think before they put others down, or share some online story without verifying it. I don't know when calling people names became vogue, but it's gotta stop. This is a good educational opportunity for them."

"How awesome of me to provide it," Steph deadpanned.

"Remember, you're also demonstrating what to do when we make a mistake." Carrie took a sip of her water. "That's another lesson people—not just kids—need to learn or relearn."

"True." Steph pointed to a starred item on her list. "I also spoke with the local radio station, and they said they'd give us a half-hour slot on Monday." She glanced at Kyle. "If you can get off work."

"I'll do it." Thankfully, Pastor Mitch was a hundred percent in his corner and had encouraged him to do whatever was necessary to save Dad's reputation.

"Good. They said they'd seen my viral vlog, but not the apology."

"Not a surprise." Bad news always traveled faster, it seemed. Kyle glanced at Steph's list of crossed-off items. "If you have time, I have a few items to add."

"Okay." She grabbed her pen off the table and held it over the notepad. "What've you got?" Her voice trembled, contradicting the confidence she was attempting to show.

"This Sunday, my pastor invited us to speak at all three services. He's been trying to deal with gossip in the church since he began. Figured this would be a good way to curtail it. At least for now."

"I'll be there." Her voice hitched just a bit, but he heard it. "What church?"

"New Hope on Second Avenue." He turned and met her gaze. "I want you to know how much I appreciate you doing this. I know it's not easy for you."

She shrugged and looked away, pretending it was no big deal, but he knew better. "You do what you have to do to make things better when you mess up."

"I agree, which is why I'm—"

The waitress appeared at their table with a tray of food, interrupting Kyle. All the better because some things were best said without a crowd.

While they ate, conversation turned to work and families and kids and their brother's wedding. In the midst of this turmoil, he loved the normalcy of the conversation. Even though he was an outsider, he'd been welcomed into their circle.

To think he could have had this for the past ten years instead of…

Nope. No condemnation.

They ate their burgers, and the sisters left, hurrying home to their own daughters. Angie hung around way too long, probably hoping he'd take off first, but he managed to wait her out. At last she left, and then he made his offer.

"Take a walk with me?"

"Do you think that's a good idea?"

He scratched the side of his face, wondering that himself. "It's just a walk."

She chuckled. "Yeah. Just."

"That's all it has to be."

"Hmm."

He stood and offered his hand to help her up, and she gave him the stink eye.

"Fine." He raised both hands. "I was just being polite."

"There's that word again. Just. Sounds like ulterior motives to me."

"Just a talk and walk."

"Just."

He dropped his chin to his chest. It seemed he couldn't speak without that word, so he zipped his lips and gestured toward the exit door. He followed her, his hands stuck in his pockets.

She led the way to the Riverwalk, and they walked side

by side down the concrete path filled with other moonlight walkers, exchanging no words.

Once they'd passed the bulk of the crowd, he gestured to a bench facing the river. "Care to sit?"

Without answering, she aimed for the bench and sat, crossing her arms over her chest.

Okay then.

He sat beside her, resting his elbows on his knees while looking out over the river. Like burgers, a river had been a part of their first date. They'd enjoyed their lunch while watching the Mississippi's high spring waters rush past. He'd brought his guitar, and with the river providing a musical undercurrent, they'd harmonized together for the first time. He'd fallen for her that night.

"Remember our first date?" She uncrossed her arms and rubbed her hands over her jeans.

"Was just thinking about it."

"Just?"

He groaned, but smiled. "Yes, just."

"You played guitar."

"We sang."

"You wrote a song."

"Uh-uh. *We* wrote the song. I wrote the melody, you came up with the lyrics. Teamwork."

"And then you wrote my name wrong in your notes."

"Who spells Stephenie with three E's?"

"Blame my dad. He said I was unique from the beginning."

"You still are."

"Kyle..." She pushed off the bench and crossed her arms again. "I don't want to do this." She walked to the edge of the path and stared at the river.

You started it came to mind, but he thought better of it, thank goodness. "You're right." He joined her on the path, his hands digging deep into his pockets. "I was sitting there trying to figure out how to apologize."

"Oh, it's really easy, actually. Only two words. I'm sorry."

"Would that really be enough? Serious question."

She dragged the toe of her tennis shoe through the grass, which was just beginning to turn green. "I don't know. Serious answer."

"Okay, then. Can we sit again?"

She shrugged and trudged back to the bench.

He sat beside her, his gaze following the river. "I'm sorry for messing up with you. I wish I'd have been stronger."

Silence.

"And I'm sorry I didn't understand your silence. I was ashamed, especially being the church's music minister, and I thought you hated me, so I gave you a way out. When you didn't fight it..."

"I didn't fight because I thought you'd gotten what you wanted from me, and I was right. A month later, I caught you and Ronnie going at it."

He closed his eyes, hating the visual. "She was an opportunist, and I was an idiot. You and I were done, she was the pastor's daughter—"

"The pastor's *hot* daughter."

He squirmed at that. Yeah, *hot* had been the word to

describe Ronnie all right. No red-blooded guy didn't notice her. Once Steph was out of the way, Ronnie had come on to him, and it didn't take long before they were in the sack together. He'd rationalized it, telling himself that if the pastor's daughter did it, it must be okay.

"We moved in together, and the pastor accepted me as his son." He bent over and yanked grass from the ground. "He never told me what I was doing with his daughter was wrong. Everyone just—"

"Just…"

"Would you stop it?" He ran his hands through hair that used to be highlighted and gelled. "I'm trying to be honest here."

"I'm sorry."

He sighed. "I missed you, you know. After worship, I'd look for you. It took me a whole year to realize you weren't coming back and that I had to settle for second best."

"Really?" Cynicism bled through the word.

"I'm being serious. The pastor loved me. The staff loved me. The congregation loved me. I loved the attention, or thought I did. Career-wise, I was on a high. I knew how to pray, 'It's not about me,' but I'd forgotten how to live that. And yes, I'd settled for Ronnie. Half the time we were just two people living in the same home, sharing the same bed, but that was it. I was too self-absorbed to focus on *us*. Besides, I always told myself we weren't married, and that we'd never made a commitment. If things didn't work out, I'd move."

"Sounds like a sad way to live."

He laughed wryly. "Tell me about it. Almost two years ago, Ronnie came to me and said she was pregnant. I was over-the-moon ecstatic for half a second, hoping that would make the two of us happy, but then she punctuated her announcement with a second one that said she was leaving me for the good doctor."

"So, Evie isn't yours?"

"Oh, she's mine. Ronnie emphasized that she hadn't slept with him. Yet. Said she wouldn't cheat on me. I actually laughed at her, asked how she could be in love with someone else if she hadn't cheated on me."

"I'm sorry."

"Don't be sorry for me. I brought that on myself. Evie's the one I feel sorry for. The actions of two selfish adults means she'll be shuttled between us until she leaves home. It was that realization that made me take another look at True North, and I realized they weren't true, nor were they pointing north, and for my spiritual health, I needed to get out of there. I got that job at New Hope and Pastor Mitch showed me where true north really was."

"I'm glad for you." Steph actually turned in his direction. "It's obviously made a difference."

"It has. And because of them, I've learned I have unfinished business. On Monday night I've got an appointment with Ronnie's dad. The Bible tells us that when a brother sins against us, we're to go talk to them alone."

"Like you're talking with me?"

"Exactly."

"But I'm also going to talk to him about the vandalism and Ronnie threatening a custody battle. He always liked me. I hope I can get him to battle for me."

"From what I remember of him, I wouldn't expect it."

Unfortunately, Kyle had just as much hope as Steph when it came to that pastor, but God could do miracles.

"Thanks for listening." He angled his head her direction and managed to briefly catch her eye. "I guess I say all this as an apology. I messed up with you, and that pushed me away from God, but He's welcomed me home. Hopefully, I'm a better man for it in the end."

"I think you are," she said softly and once again hugged herself.

Guess it was time to go. He stood and offered his hand. "Shall we head back?"

She stared at his hand for a second, then placed hers in his.

He helped her stand, and she quickly tugged her hand away. As expected.

Conversation stilled between the two as they walked back to the restaurant parking lot. He escorted her to her car and remained close as she unlocked then opened the door.

She started to step inside, but he touched her arm, needing to say one more thing.

"For the record, Stephenie Triple-E Winter, of all the mistakes I've made, letting go of you is the one I regret most. You've become an amazing woman. If you ever do get married, that guy'll be lucky to have you."

Her lips opened slightly, then quickly closed as she sat down.

He backed away and watched her until she drove off. Yeah, she'd become an amazing woman.

And he'd forever blown his chance with her.

Steph licked her lips as she drove off. There was something sorely wrong with her. The whole night she'd waited—no, wanted him to take her hand. And then at the car, if he'd kissed her goodnight, she wouldn't have complained. What was wrong with her? She might as well forfeit her Single and Staying Strong & Independent card right now.

She glanced in the rearview mirror before pulling out of the parking lot.

He still stood there, looking downright handsome, and so different from the young man who'd worked so hard at being popular that it stripped him of who he was. If he were any other man, she might have...

Might have what? Invited him back to her place for a cocktail and breakfast?

She gulped. That was the old Steph. She was the redeemed version. All she knew now was she couldn't wait to be done with all the talks scheduled for Sunday and Monday. Not only did speaking scare her to death, but that much time spent with the redeemed Kyle Stevens was going to do a number on her heart.

Chapter Eleven

Steph sat near the back of the sanctuary, her gaze up front on Kyle leading the congregants in worship. The decibel level was far less than at True North. She could even hear people sing. Usually she loved to sing along, but hearing so many others join in worship both floored and muted her. And it stirred her in a way she'd never before experienced. This was genuine love for their Savior.

Or maybe, for the first time, her heart was prepared for worship.

That song moved into another she knew by heart, so she closed her eyes and sang along, shoving their upcoming *The Rumor Stops Here* talk to the back of her mind as she worshiped.

The song finished, the congregants sat, the pastor took the pulpit, and her nervousness resumed with a bam. Suddenly she was sweating, nearly hyperventilating, her throat felt clogged, and her heart was racing faster than her vlog had gone viral.

She couldn't do this. She hugged herself trying to chase

the chills, but it wasn't working. If she went up on that stage, or altar, or whatever it was called, she'd throw up. No doubt about it. How had she agreed to do this once, much less three times today, and then tomorrow too?

But Kyle couldn't do it alone.

The words wouldn't carry weight if she didn't say them.

Oh, God, I can't do this!

"How are you doing?"

Steph startled and shook her head. She didn't even have a voice for Kyle as he sat beside her.

"You'll be fine," he whispered. "Just be you, and I'll be right beside you the whole time."

If only she could be as calm as he was. If she couldn't make it through one talk today, how would she make it through tomorrow? They were slated to speak to three classrooms and appear on the local radio station. Following that, Kyle had an appointment with the pastor from True North.

Once all the speaking was done, she'd be drained for the rest of the week. She was exhausted now just thinking about it. And even when it was over, they weren't guaranteed they'd make a difference.

Oh, what had she gotten herself into? All because she hadn't adhered to the 3R's: Regard * Research * React. If she had to become a public speaker to make it up to Mr. Stevens, well, that was exactly what she'd do, even if she looked and sounded like a fool.

"Ready?"

She startled as Kyle got up.

This soon? Nope, she wasn't ready at all, and couldn't convince her legs to stand.

"You've got this, Trip."

He offered his hand, and with a gulp she took it and forced herself from the chair. Walking with him, she gripped his hand until his fingers turned white, but he said nothing.

He led her out the back of the sanctuary and through some secret hallway to the side of the pulpit area. Her antiperspirant had worn off an hour ago—it was a wonder Kyle could even bear standing beside her.

The pastor was saying something about rumors and listening and kindness, and then he said Kyle's name followed by hers.

"You've got this," Kyle whispered again. "And I'm not going to leave your side. Just imagine you're talking to your phone, doing a video."

She nodded and followed him onto the stage or whatever traditional churches called this area. Two stools were set to the right of the pulpit. Kyle gestured for her to sit while someone handed him a microphone.

Her mouth went cotton dry, and she swore the congregation could see her heart palpitating right out of her chest.

Then Kyle was talking, thanking the pastor for giving them the floor.

Focus, Steph, focus. She concentrated on breathing while listening to Kyle's introduction.

"I met Stephenie about twelve years ago when I was a

new worship minister at my previous church. Through circumstances neither of us chose, we've been brought back together, and God has taught us a lot. Our hope, our belief is that God will take our experience and use it for good. Steph, would you care to elaborate?"

He handed her the microphone, and it slipped in her sweaty palms, but he caught it for her and gave her a reassuring glance, mouthing again, "You've got this."

She licked her lips and smiled, or she tried to smile, anyway. "Thank you, Kyle and Pastor Mitch, for welcoming me." Somehow the words leaked from her mouth. She looked out at the congregation, imagining she was talking to her phone and forced out more words. "In the social media world, I'm known as the *Be Bold & Sassi* vlogger, and my vlog has had a measure of success. A few weeks ago, a vlog I posted went viral—some of you may have seen it."

Her voice grew raspier with each sentence, and someone handed her a glass of water. She took a drink then continued talking, repeating what she'd practiced with Kyle. "In it, I accused a man of stalking children. The problem is, I was wrong, very wrong. The man was—is completely innocent, and speaking without thinking or researching in advance has greatly harmed this man's reputation. That man is Kyle's dad."

She looked at Kyle, who nodded, but sadness filled his eyes. "So, we're here today to get the truth out. We want the truth to go viral."

"Amen," someone said from the congregation.

That gave her fuel to keep going. "We also want to use

this opportunity to share some wisdom we've learned on this journey. Well-renowned missionary Amy Carmichael once said, 'Let nothing be said about anyone unless it passes through the three sieves: Is it true? Is it kind? Is it necessary?' My vlog post didn't even make it through that first sieve. Yes, I'd believed it was necessary to get the word out, but first I should have verified the truth."

Kyle held out his hand, offering to take the microphone, and she gladly handed it over.

"We both have realized how often in our world today Amy Carmichael's wisdom is ignored. Think about your interactions on social media. Are they true? Kind? Necessary? Personally, I know mine haven't always been. What about when we speak in our daily interactions? Ephesians 4:29 says, 'Do not let any unwholesome talk come out of your mouths, but only what is helpful for building others up according to their needs, that it may benefit those who listen.' And many other Bible verses speak to being a good listener. Will that good listener be you?"

Will that be her?

From now on, Steph would be careful about what she shared. She reached for the microphone again, to Kyle's astonishment and hers.

She had one more little nugget to share. "For those of you like me who use mnemonic devices to remember things, just remember the 3R's: Regard, Research, and React. Regard means listen. Then Research to determine the truth. Only then do you React—that's your decision of whether what you're saying or doing is kind and necessary. If it isn't, please reconsider."

She looked out at the congregation, who had been kind to her when she didn't deserve it. She'd brought injury upon someone they loved, yet they listened without judgment. They'd offered her amazing mercy.

"Thank you for your time today. I do hope you realize how sorry I am for starting this rumor, for hurting Kyle and his father, and I hope that you will join with us in spreading the truth. God bless you all."

She'd made it through the day.

Steph sat in the passenger seat of Kyle's Subaru, silently doing a little victory dance as he drove away from the last school engagement, heading for his old church. Her sister's school, like the church, was north of the Twin Cities, so it made sense to schedule the times close together, even if that meant more time spent with Kyle.

Although, it really hadn't been bad.

Truthfully, she'd enjoyed it.

But seeing her former church again was something she'd hoped never to do. She'd make it through though, just as she'd made it through all the talks. Students, for the most part, had listened. She hadn't had a single panic attack throughout the day. She'd had a few moments of thinking "I can't do this" but Kyle had nudged her on, encouraging, not pushing.

Going live on the radio was easier than speaking at school, as it was more like doing her vlog.

Now they had to wait to see if all their work bore fruit. Unfortunately, it wouldn't happen overnight, and that hurt her heart. If Ray moved to Florida or if Kyle lost Evie in a custody battle, she didn't know if she could forgive herself.

These past two days spent with him had proven beyond a doubt that he was a changed man, and she couldn't bear to see him hurt.

Or was there more to her feelings than that?

No going there. Not right now. Just focus on the fact that they'd nailed their talks today, so they'd done all they could.

"How are you doing?" He tapped his fingers on the steering wheel, probably to a tune that was playing in his mind.

"Like a...champion." Yeah, that fit.

He grinned. "You rocked it, you know. We've done our part, the rest we leave up to God." His smile faded a bit. No doubt, the threat of a custody battle darkened his mind.

"I'm praying for you." And she was. Somehow the words didn't sound as trite as they used to.

"I appreciate it."

Hopefully, this meeting with the pastor would work to convince Ronnie to not file a custody suit. Though, Kyle didn't sound convinced.

Moments later, the church where they'd met came into view. The place had been a massive structure ten years ago, and it looked as if more had been added on.

Just like that, her feelings of celebration vanished. A church shouldn't be a joy thief, but this building was. Thankfully, the weather was warm enough for her to sit outside with her guitar, like she used to do. That was a good memory, at least.

They arrived at the church and parked and Kyle just sat there, his eyes closed. Composing himself? No, this new Kyle was probably praying.

"Time to head in," he said, trying to sound chipper, but failing.

"You've got this." She gave him a thumbs-up. He'd nudged and encouraged her over the last two days, the least she could do was return the favor.

"Yeah, God and I do. Thanks." He pushed the ignition button, turning off the car. "You'll be fine out here?"

"Much better than inside."

"Well, if you need anything from the car." He tossed her the keyless remote. "I don't plan to be long, but the man can be, ahem, long-winded."

"And I'll be under a tree." She retrieved her guitar from the backseat then locked up the vehicle as Kyle headed inside. She had her doubts that the pastor would listen, especially when it came to his daughter, but she could hope.

And pray.

She reached a tree with good shade, sat down and leaned against it, then wrapped Kyle in prayer.

Kyle wiped his sweaty palms on his jeans as he waited in the lobby outside Pastor Dean Whitmer's office door. He hadn't seen the man since getting the job at New Hope. Hopefully, they'd still get along, but there were no guarantees, not when the man's granddaughter's life was being tossed about. They both wanted what was best for Evie. The problem was, would they agree on what "the best" was?

At last, the office door opened, and Pastor Dean released one of his famous grins. That was good, right? "How are you doing, Kyle? So good to see you again. Come on in."

Kyle released the breath he hadn't realized he'd been holding and stepped into the office. It wasn't a big space, like some would expect. It actually reflected a humble man.

A new picture hung on the wall behind the desk, that made Kyle's blood boil. Ronnie with her fiancé, who held Evie.

"Nice portrait, wouldn't you say?"

Kyle didn't answer, but heard the door click shut behind him.

"Have a seat." The man's voice suddenly lost its welcoming tone, but Kyle obeyed him. The pastor rounded the desk, sat, and folded his hands on what looked like sermon notes. The grin remained on his face, but somehow it appeared sinister now. The man gestured to the portrait of Ronnie's new family. "Lovely engagement picture, isn't it?"

Really? Well, guess that told Kyle where he ranked with the good pastor. He puffed out a long breath and responded in a way that hopefully showed he didn't care what Ronnie did. "Good for them." Yeah, he and Ronnie were over, but still, they'd spent nearly eight years together as a couple. Those weren't easy years to throw away, and part of him still grieved the loss of the relationship, as shallow as it had been.

"Yes, I'm quite happy for them. Gavin will provide well."

As if that was all that mattered. Kyle refused to respond.

Pastor Dean reclined in his office chair, his hands folded over a slightly bulging stomach. "Veronica also tells me you've gotten yourself in a bit of trouble. I hope you haven't come to me to bail you out."

Seriously? After all the years he'd given the church, after the years he'd spent thinking of this man as a second father, that was all the regard the man had for him?

His rudeness actually gave Kyle the nerve to address the pastor forthright. "That's part of why I needed to meet with you today, but first I have to ask you, father to father, why you didn't respect your daughter enough to tell me to get married or get lost?"

A frown replaced the creepy smile. "Son, do you really believe that I supported your shacking up with my daughter? That was her choice, and she's an adult, and was capable of making her own choices whether I agreed with them or not."

Kyle couldn't argue with that. His dad would have said the same thing. Actually, Dad and Mom had spoken those words.

"But when I met Gavin." Pastor Dean nodded toward the engagement picture. "I knew I'd found the right single man for her, a man I'd be glad to call *son*, and sent him her way."

Kyle blinked, taking that in. Pastor Dean was behind his and Ronnie's breakup. Unbelievable. And he stood behind the pulpit every week, preaching from God's Word? No wonder the Word seemed to fall on deaf ears in the True North congregation.

"Wow. I have nothing to say." Kyle shook his head.

"Then I'll see you out."

Kyle began to stand, but stopped midway, and sat back down. "Actually, I do need to say something." Clearly, pleading for the man's help in the looming custody battle would be a waste of time, but there was also the matter of him approaching the Christian who'd wronged him to make it right. Before speaking, he ran his thoughts through Steph's 3R's—regard, research, and react—and decided this was the perfect opportunity to speak the truth in love.

The man sighed, clearly annoyed now, and no longer donning the "Good Pastor" mask. "Make it short. I have another appointment."

"No problem." Kyle sat up straight. "In all my years at True North, not once did anyone in this church come to me and tell me I was sinning, even flaunting that sin, all because society says it's okay. But my behavior wasn't okay, just as a Christian church that doesn't uphold Biblical teaching is wrong."

"Watch it." The man's face began to grow red.

But Kyle was just beginning.

Steph looked toward the church entry. No sign of Kyle yet. It was taking longer than she'd anticipated. Whether that boded well for him or not, she didn't know. What she did know was that she needed to continue in prayer.

A car door slamming grabbed her attention, and she glanced across the parking lot. Just two guys getting out of a black pickup.

Wait. She did a double take. They weren't just a couple of guys. She sat up and focused on them. Weren't they the brothers she'd met that night at the bar with Angie? Nah, not way up here. That would be too coincidental.

A shiver ran down her spine. Yes, definitely too coincidental. She watched them enter the church, then glanced at their pickup. Should she? Her brother would likely wring her neck, but she got up, leaving her guitar by the tree, and jogged toward the pickup, with frequent glances at the church entry. When she got close enough, she snapped a couple of shots with her phone that included the license plate.

She glanced inside the cab. Nothing unusual. She checked the truck bed.

A box of spray paint cans.

She gulped but quickly snapped a photo. The cans proved nothing.

But they could mean everything. That was for the cops to decide.

The brothers came out of the church.

Her heart galloping, she backed away.

Should she return to her tree? No, that would be too

obvious. Instead, she strode purposely toward the sidewalk leading into the church, hoping they'd buy her being here as a mere coincidence.

Her heart still pumping furiously, she approached the two and stopped quickly, slapping a hand to her heart. "Don't I know you guys?"

They also ground to a quick halt. Both pairs of eyes widened.

The brother who'd played the wise older brother in the bar stammered, "I, uh…"

She snapped her fingers. "Oh, I know. I met you guys a few weeks ago down in Apple Valley, right? Imagine seeing you guys here! A friend of mine recommended this church, and I was meeting him here. Do you go here?"

A fake smile, the one he'd used when hitting on her and Angie, formed on the other brother's face. "Imagine that. But I don't think you'll like this church."

"Sad to hear that. Well, good to see you guys again. Maybe we'll meet up some other time." She strode past them, aiming for the entry door, praying they'd bought her pretense.

Kyle stood in the open door to the pastor's office, watching the man tug at his shirt collar as if grasping for air.

"You're still here?" Pastor Dean rasped.

"I have one more thing to say." But what had those goons said to him? He was obviously flustered, and Kyle was likely going to add to it. Once he had his say, he'd wipe the dust off his shoes and go home.

"I don't recall you being this bold when you dated my daughter."

"Yeah, well, life circumstances change people. I'm no longer someone's patsy."

"Fine. Say what you have to say, then leave. I've had enough to deal with today."

"And I have, too. Your daughter is threatening to file for full custody if the dirtbags who sprayed nasty things over my dad's house aren't caught. So, yeah, you grow a bit bold when you're defending your daughter, as you well know."

"Yes, I do. I would do anything for her." The pastor closed his eyes, and his back hunched. "I'm listening."

Kyle prayed for the right words. "I know I'm just a music minister. I haven't had the years of seminary training that you have, but it seems to me a Christian church should be preaching and upholding Christian values. That's not what I experienced at True North. This church is not pointing toward Jesus."

His phone buzzed, and he instinctively reached for it.

"Guess that's your cue to leave." Pastor Dean opened his eyes and sat up straight, regaining his authority. He gestured toward the door. "Look at your phone on your way out, because you're done here."

Yes, he was.

Kyle headed out the door.

"For your sake..."

Kyle looked back.

"I hope they catch the two crooks who did this to you and your father. He's a good man, and so are you."

Now he was really confused. Kyle left the office and closed the door behind him. He'd had his say, he'd confronted the head of the church who was clearly not remorseful. Maybe that would come over time. If God could perform miracles with Kyle's heart, he could work on anyone.

He pulled out his phone to check the message.

From Steph:

– Sorry, I need to get going –

Guess the text had been his cue. He hurried from the church and glanced toward the tree Steph had sat under.

She was pacing across the lawn, guitar slung across her back, her shoulders hunched as if weighted down.

"Steph?" He jogged toward her. "What's up?"

She looked past him, first over the left shoulder, then the right, then directly in his eyes. "I think I know who vandalized your place."

"I don't want to talk about it here." Steph grabbed Kyle's arm and practically dragged him toward his crossover. She wanted out of here before the brothers figured out her ruse and returned.

She laid the guitar on the backseat, then got in beside Kyle.

"Where to?" He started the vehicle.

"The police station in Northfield." That was what her brother would tell her to do, at least she thought that's what he'd tell her to do.

"Why?" He accelerated. "What happened?"

She filled him in on meeting the brothers.

"I don't like this." His fingers white knuckled on the steering wheel. "Two men went in to talk with Pastor Dean while I was there." His face suddenly grew as white as his knuckles. "No…" the words breathed from his mouth.

"What?"

"Pastor Dean said something that I didn't catch right away, but now that I think about it, when I left, he said he hoped they caught the two crooks." He shot a quick glance at Steph. "There's no way he would have known the police were looking at two people."

He gulped and his jaw tightened as the crossover sped up on the freeway. "Call Dad, tell him to meet us at the police station."

Steph knew exactly what he was thinking: Pastor Dean may not have spray painted Ray's house, but he paid off people who did, and that meant any of them could be in danger.

Chapter Twelve

*K*yle glanced in the rearview mirror while going at a snail's pace through the Twin Cities on a freeway narrowed with construction. He'd been eyeing a pickup a few vehicles back for a while. Every turn Kyle had taken, that truck seemed to follow. He could be paranoid, but this didn't feel right.

He didn't want to frighten Steph, but they needed to make a move, and he couldn't protect them without her assistance.

"Steph." He kept his eye on the pickup and tried to speak in a cool tone. "I'd like you to find the closest police department."

"What? Why?"

"Don't turn around, just look in your side mirror." Out of the corner of his eye, he watched her look. "See that pickup two vehicles behind us? Does it look familiar?"

He waited for her answer as he inched forward.

"It could be, but half the pickups in Minnesota are black."

Including his dad's. "This pickup also has two men, and

it's been trailing us since Roseville, at least."

She started jabbing at her phone. "You really think this could be the brothers?"

"I'd rather err on the side of safety."

"Right." She clamped her phone in the clip in his vent. "Five minutes to the nearest station."

"Thanks." In a mile, he'd be getting off the freeway to the right, but didn't want to give that away, so he remained in the center lane for now. He'd just have to do some fancy driving when it came to that exit, and he'd likely make a lot of drivers mad.

The traffic sped up a titch, but his heartbeat raced as if it were driving the Indy 500. Half a mile to go. The cars in the right lane drove bumper-to-bumper. He'd need a lot of luck squeezing between them.

Quarter mile.

Eighth of a mile.

He checked his side mirror and held his breath as he slipped between two semis, a very good hiding place, though the driver in back of him threw an obscene gesture.

The exit ramp was on his right. Nearly passing.

Kyle swerved onto the ramp directly in front of another vehicle. Steph squealed. The other driver laid on his horn.

"You're making lots of friends." Steph laughed nervously.

"Yep." He glanced in the rearview mirror and wanted to curse. "They're following."

"We're almost there."

The vehicle behind him turned off.

"They're right behind us."

She glanced in the mirror and gasped. "It is them."

"I knew it." He pounded on the steering wheel, wanting to go faster, but traffic was nearly at a halt. "I'm taking a detour."

He spun the wheel to the right and squealed onto a side street squished with cars on both sides. The pickup followed, but had trouble fitting between all the cars, slowing him down. Kyle took the next left. From here it was a straight shot.

The pickup rounded the corner and zoomed toward them.

Just one and a half blocks.

One block.

The pickup came up behind them fast, nearly hugging their bumper.

Half a block. Kyle laid on his horn. This close to the police station, that should grab attention.

The pickup drew back then swerved around them, rushing down the block.

Kyle and Steph exhaled at the same time while turning into the police station parking lot. He'd barely parked before Steph was out of the car, running toward the station. Kyle ran up alongside her. Only once they were inside the building did his heart begin to slow.

Steph strode right up to the reception desk. "I need to speak to an officer immediately. We've been threatened, and we have evidence of a crime."

A minute later, they were seated in a small room, spilling

out the entire story to Officers Greene and Donaldson, which was collaborated by the Northfield Police—Dad had been there for several minutes already. She shared the pictures of the pickup and the spray cans in the bed, plus one Kyle didn't know she'd taken.

The closeup of the brothers in the pickup nearly grazing their bumper proved their story.

"Thanks for bringing this to us." Officer Greene stood and offered his hand. "We'll get right on it."

"We appreciate it." Steph beat him to the handshake. "And I'll be talking with my brother, Officer Daniel Winter on the Rochester PD as well."

The officers didn't seem impressed, but in this case, it didn't hurt to mention connections who would help keep this case in the forefront. Kyle wanted this solved now.

For his daughter.

His dad.

And Stephenie.

He wanted her to have the peace of this being behind her, but until the brothers were caught—they shouldn't be that far away yet—her safety, all their safety was in jeopardy, which meant none of them could go home.

They walked out of the station to his crossover, and he locked the doors immediately upon sitting down.

"You okay?"

She nodded. "Angry more than anything. I just want to go home and forget all of this."

"We can't go home." He started the vehicle.

"Why not?"

"With those goons on the loose?"

"Oh."

"We'll find a hotel and—"

"Uh-uh. Not happening, buddy."

"I was going to say, 'get separate rooms.'"

"Oh."

He laughed, hoping to get her to loosen up a bit. "You keep saying that."

"Well, you keep making good points that I didn't think of." She even grinned.

"First time for everything." He stared ahead at the police station, wondering if they really were "getting right on it."

"Then I have the perfect plan." She took out her phone. "Pick up your dad, and we'll all stay at Mom and Dad's."

"They won't mind?"

"Well, they'll probably have you sleep in the pole shed."

"There is that."

"But your dad and I will be welcome. You might even get breakfast."

"Then what are we waiting for?"

She held up her phone. "I'm going to give them fair warning, first."

Steph plopped down on the living room couch and groaned. She had never felt so exhausted. Had it just been earlier today that she and Kyle had conquered schools and radio?

Now, after being followed, stopping at not one, but two police stations, and then spilling her guts to her parents, she was fried. And full. Oh, her mom could cook. Steph could too, she just didn't enjoy it.

"Oh, that was good." Kyle sat on the far side of the couch and patted his stomach. "I haven't eaten like that since…" He laid his head back. "Probably since the last time I was here."

"And then you turned vegan."

"What was I thinking? That beef stroganoff was unreal." He sat up and grinned. "We'll find out soon enough if mine was laced with arsenic."

That made her laugh.

She scooched a little closer to Kyle and held out her hand. "I think they've forgiven you."

He looked down at her hand then at her face. "And what about you?"

"I…" She stared across the living room, out the open window at the porch swing they used to sit on and make music. Was it wrong to still want that? A chill came through that window, and she rubbed her arms.

"Come here." He gestured to the spot beside him.

"I haven't said *I forgive you* yet."

"Do you want to?" His eyes searched hers.

And she felt laid bare. "I do," she whispered.

He held out his hand. "Then come here. I promise I won't bite."

"And I can't promise you this means anything other than 'I'm chilly.'"

"Well then." He removed a blanket from the back of the couch and held it up.

This was nearly as nerve-wracking as having those goons chase them, but she slid over, and he wrapped her in the blanket. Then she rested against his shoulder. She couldn't seem to help herself.

"That's better." He wrapped his arms around her and kissed the top of her head.

She closed her eyes and sighed. Yes, this was definitely better.

But once they were safe, and adrenaline rushes weren't tainting their decisions, would it remain good?

"Seriously, Steph?"

She shook herself awake, too cozy on the couch in Kyle's arms, and found herself face to face with her not-so-little kid brother.

"I come back from my honeymoon and hear all about this trouble you've stirred up."

Kyle's arms fell away as he sat up, forcing her to sit up as well.

"I've never been prouder of your sister." Kyle squeezed her shoulder and let go too soon.

"Coming from you, that doesn't mean a lot." Daniel sat in the wingback chair across from them, but leaned forward, his forearms resting on his knees.

"Uh-uh." Steph wagged her finger at Daniel. "Even after what I did, this man has stood beside me, forgiven me, so don't you dare harp on him."

"I don't want to see you hurt again." Daniel's gaze fired at Kyle.

"I guess that's my choice, isn't it?" She leaned toward her brother.

"Hmph." He sat back.

"Hmph back." She wrinkled her nose and stuck out her tongue.

"Man, you two still fight like teenagers." Kyle chuckled behind her.

"And I could still beat him up, too." She balled her hands in a boxing pose.

Both men laughed at that. Good. She needed to ease the tension and get to the heart of why Daniel was here—she glanced at her watch—at six thirty in the morning. The guy was never up this early, and he had a new wife, so that meant he had information.

"What can you tell us?" She moved a cushion's-width away from Kyle so she could focus.

Daniel looked directly at Kyle. "Turns out your old father-in-law isn't such a nice guy."

"Not a surprise." Kyle didn't correct the father-in-law part. "Is he behind the vandalism somehow?"

"He *was*." Daniel grinned. "Now he's behind bars."

Whoa.

She heard Kyle blow out a long breath, and that tugged at her heart, but she'd deal with that emotional part later.

Right now, she wanted facts. "So, he did hire the brothers."

"Well, not brothers, but yeah. He paid them to vandalize Mr. Stevens' home. The Richfield police picked up the two shortly after you guys left the station last night, and they sang like canaries."

"He did all this because he didn't want me to have custody," Kyle's voice was barely above a whisper.

"Afraid so. Your ex showed him Steph's vlog with your dad in it. She, of course, recognized him right away, then she also recognized Steph as the former girlfriend." Daniel looked between the two. "Please tell me you're still the 'former girlfriend.'"

She glanced at Kyle, and he shrugged. That wasn't a no or a yes. "I'll tell you that's none of your business."

"Fine, but if you hurt her again, I won't take it so nice." He hiked up his pant leg just enough to reveal a gun. "Got that?"

Kyle gulped and raised his hands. "Loud and clear."

"Stop being a jerk." Steph wanted to swat her little brother.

"I suppose that's what Rita would tell me, too." He grinned at the mention of his new wife.

"One question for you, though." Actually, she had more than one, but it was a start. "When I met the so-called brothers at the bar, was that just coincidence?"

"Nope." Daniel sat back in the chair and rested an ankle over his knee. "They were doing some recon on you just to make sure you were Kyle's ex. Once that was confirmed, they got the green light from the so-called pastor.

Apparently, he said he'd do anything for his daughter. Even breaking the law."

"We're safe to go home?" Kyle stood and started folding the blanket he'd covered both of them in.

"You are."

"I'll wake Dad. Give him the good news." Kyle placed the blanket on the back of the couch and climbed the stairs leading to the guest bedroom on the second floor, leaving her alone with her finger-pointing little brother.

"Don't say it." She jabbed a finger his way.

"Say what?" Daniel raised his hands, palms up as if to say he didn't have a clue of what she was talking about. The jerk.

"That Kyle isn't good enough for me."

"You said it, not me."

She huffed. "Well maybe he is, maybe he isn't." She looked toward the stairway. "But I'm willing to take that chance." Her stomach even did a little flutter thinking about it, the first time since the break-up she'd felt like this about someone.

She prayed she wasn't making the same mistake twice.

Chapter Thirteen

Kyle whistled as he drove onto the street of his new home. Behind him, Steph slept, and beside him, his dad had been quiet. This had been a lot to place on a man. Kyle still prayed his father would decide not to move. He'd missed too much father-son time already.

But he'd worry about that later. Right now, he couldn't wait to get home and sleep in his own bed. It was only noon, but he'd likely sleep all day. Thankfully, Pastor Mitch had encouraged him to take the day off. Kyle doubted he'd have been able to focus on work today.

But tomorrow, he'd go in refreshed, ready to tackle the day.

He pulled alongside Steph's car that had been parked there since yesterday morning.

Yesterday?

Had it really only been yesterday that they'd gone on their school and radio tour? It seemed like forever ago.

He thanked God, once again, for revealing the truth and then prayed that the truth would go viral just as the lie had.

The car was barely in park before Dad had the door open. "It's been a long night, I'm gonna head home."

He still sounded exhausted, and that worried Kyle. He started to follow after his father.

"I'll go." Steph briefly touched his arm. "I think he needs a woman's touch right now. I'll get him settled, then I'll come say goodbye."

Kyle wouldn't argue with that. She'd probably bring Dad cookies and coffee and fry up a pound of bacon. Huh, maybe Kyle needed his own woman's touch.

He trudged to his home that would be empty. He unlocked the door, then opened it and listened to silence. Oh, how he longed to hear Evie's soprano squeal and then have her pudgy little arms circle his neck and squeeze him with a hug that told him he was the best daddy in the world.

Tomorrow he'd make the call to Ronnie. Today he was too exhausted to be civil, and facing her meant he had to be kind. After what her father had put them through, his kindness meter was on empty.

He checked his fridge for something to whip up quickly, something Steph would like. Did she still like grilled peanut butter and banana sandwiches? That used to be a staple of theirs. He pulled out his griddle and melted butter on it, then buttered both sides of four slices of bread, and topped two with chunky peanut butter and banana slices.

He started frying those, then began setting the table when he heard a knock on his door. He hurried to the door and flung it open expecting to see Steph.

"Ronnie?" And Evie!

"Dada!"

He blinked away tears as Evie reached for him. "Hey, baby girl, Dada's missed you so much." He took her in his arms and had to hold himself back from gripping her too tight. He dug his nose into her hair, memorizing that fruity scent of her baby shampoo.

"Something's burning."

What? Oh, his sandwiches!

"Here." He handed Evie back to Ronnie then hurried to the stove, too late to save his lunch. "Drat." And he was really craving that sandwich. Once Ronnie left, hopefully all by herself, then he'd start new sandwiches, maybe introduce his daughter to them. It was never too early to educate your kids, right?

"Sorry about that." Ronnie held on to Evie and perused the room. "Is it childproofed?"

"It's safe," he answered dryly. Of course, it was childproofed.

"Good." She lowered their daughter to the ground, and she immediately toddled toward the corner where the bright-red crate held all her toys. "I need to talk to you."

"It can't wait? It's been a long couple of days."

"I know." She sniffled, then dabbed at her eyes.

And he was Mr. Insensitive. Her dad had just been jailed, the least he could do was show some sympathy.

"I'm sorry. That was rude." He nodded to the couch, where they both sat. "How are you doing? How's your mom?"

"How do you think we're doing?" She wiped her eyes

again. "The man I've looked up to all my life suddenly becomes a...a criminal? I can't wrap my head around it."

"If it helps any, he was doing it for you, wanting the best for Evie, and that wasn't me apparently."

She laughed and shook her head. "Did you know Dad introduced me to Gavin?"

Kyle nodded.

"I love him, and he's a good man, but this mess, it taints everything."

He had nothing to say to that.

Again, she wiped her eyes and sat up straight. "Are you okay to take Evie now? Gavin and I, we need to work some things out."

He did his best not to look gleeful and to keep himself from doing handstands. "Of course."

"Thank you." She got up and looked at the daughter they'd created together, a gift of grace. "You're a good man, Kyle Stevens."

"I wish I'd have been better for you."

She laughed. "That makes two of us." She opened her arms.

He accepted her hug, one that said both "I'm sorry" and "Goodbye."

Then she let go.

As did he. Completely.

"I'll see you in a week?"

He nodded.

"Evie, honey, come say bye-bye to Momma."

Their daughter remained at the toy bin and just waved.

"You see how I rank." Her lips pinched together. "Take good care of her." And she stalked out the door.

Wow. Kyle scratched his head. That was weird.

He checked the time. Steph must still be over at Dad's. She probably was fixing him bacon.

"Evie, wanna go see Poppa?"

She continued to play. Oh, this child was going to take after her mother, wasn't she? He walked over to her and picked her up. She squirmed, but he held her tight as he went out the front door.

And stopped.

Steph's car was gone. She hadn't even said goodbye. He checked his phone. Nothing there either. Maybe she'd left a message with Dad.

He knocked on his dad's door then let himself in. Dad was seated in his recliner, a plate of cookies and milk on the end table beside him, and the TV tuned to baseball. Steph really did know how to mother him.

"I see Steph took care of you." He bounced Evie on his hip.

"Evelyn!" Dad got up, suddenly wide awake, and hurried to take his granddaughter. "How's my best girl?" He tickled her stomach, and the cutest laugh ever emerged. "Ronnie dropped her off?"

"Yep. Then left. She's gotta deal with her dad being in jail."

"Not an easy thing for her, I'm sure."

"But the good thing is, I now get to spend time with my best girl." He pressed kisses all over those chubby cheeks, bringing out more giggles.

"Your best girl is the one that just left."

Kyle wrinkled his nose. "Ronnie?"

"No, you goofball, Stephenie. That young woman's a keeper. I hope you don't muck things up again."

Yeah, so did he.

"Um, did she say anything before she left? She never said goodbye."

"Well that's strange." Evie gripped her poppa's finger. "She headed your way not five minutes ago."

Five minutes ago?

Uh-oh. When Ronnie was there.

She hadn't seen them hugging, had she? Would that have been enough for her to run?

He hoped not.

"But she did say something about playing guitar at the park."

Of course. He snapped his fingers. Music had always been their go-to comforter when emotions ran high. But which park? Northfield had a handful, and he didn't have time to check out them all.

"Just give the woman a call."

Duh. Kyle pulled out his phone and hit the contact labeled "Trip."

No surprise, it went right to voice mail.

"Hey, Trip, er Steph, this is Kyle. Didn't get to say goodbye. Where'd you head off to?" He hung up, knowing he wasn't going to get a return phone call. Which meant, he was going to check out all the parks in town, but he had a feeling he knew which one he'd find her at.

"Dad, I gotta go." He reached for his daughter. "Wanna go for a ride, Cadenza?" He kissed her velvet-soft cheek.

She jabbered something that Kyle took for a "yes." He held her tight as he hurried to his Subaru. It took forever to buckle her into her car seat. Already, she was a little fighter. Yeah, she took after her mother all right. Hopefully, she had some of his qualities too, and not just the bad ones.

He hurried to the park that started it all, the one Dad and Mom used to go to. The one where Steph filmed the vlog that brought them back together.

Had it? Was that what this was all about?

Guess he'd find out soon enough.

He pulled into the parking lot and stopped the engine. No sign of her car, but this wasn't the only place to park. Freeing Evie from the car seat took another five minutes, and by then she was having a full-blown meltdown. One hundred percent a Ronnie trait.

He set her down on the sidewalk, and she toddled off, her tears suddenly drier than winter air. Guess she just wanted freedom. He walked behind her, his head on a continuous swivel, looking for Steph. There was the pond. The playground.

His parents' bench.

No sign of Steph.

So, he'd guessed wrong. Maybe she wanted freedom like Evie did. Maybe Steph was making her escape from him as their adventure was over.

The faint sound of a guitar hit his ears, and he stood still.

A voice joined in, and he followed the music to a tree on the far side of the park. Off where she would have privacy, not an audience.

Duh. Of course, that was where she'd be.

He prayed she wouldn't mind him joining her.

Steph closed her eyes as her fingers strummed, trying to get the right chord for a new worship song she'd heard on the radio frequently. She sang lightly along with it, but like this entire past week, it wasn't coming easy. So, keeping her eyes closed, she laid down her guitar, spread out her hands, and just sang. She needed to sing—nothing connected her with the Father like music.

She sang the first stanza, then the second, followed by the chorus. She heard grass rustling around her but didn't care. If people thought she was strange for worshiping in this park, that was their problem.

A voice joined in on harmony, a voice she knew too well. A week ago, she'd have stopped singing and probably stalked away, but today, she relished the shared worship.

Light guitar strums underscored the music, right on key. No one had an ear like Kyle.

They sang through the bridge and the chorus, twice, then the music faded with his soft hums before stopping completely.

She didn't want to open her eyes and spoil the moment. Just them and God.

"More, Dada."

And apparently, a toddler.

She opened her eyes, and seated right in front of her was a precious toddler with a green bow clipped to what little hair she had. Beside her sat Kyle, the guitar resting on his lap.

Evie clapped. "More. More."

He kissed her tiny nose. "One minute, Cadenza."

"Wait, I thought her name was Evie."

"It is. Evelyn, actually, but I needed a pet name. Punkin, Sweetie, Hey You were already taken, but Cadenza wasn't, and since she loves doing solos, the name fit."

"Fits you."

He grinned. "Guess it does." His smile faded. "Why'd you take off? Was it Ronnie?"

"Well." She looked to the ground and watched her bare foot draw circles. "I did see the two of you hugging, and you have said you'd do anything for Evie, so..." She shrugged.

"Even if that meant getting back together with Ronnie."

She shrugged again.

"Well, since Ronnie got married this past weekend, that would—"

"Married?"

"Yeah. Her dad's idea. He told me when I barged in on him yesterday. He thought it would help sway the judge for custody purposes."

"Wow." She hadn't cared for the pastor, but this? She never imagined he'd stoop to the levels he had this past week. "I'm sorry, I know you liked the guy."

"I had on blinders, but they're fully off now. I see him for who he is, a very broken man in need of a true relationship with God. I see my past choices as someone looking for approval, but never looking in the right place." He took her hand. "I see you as a woman I hurt terribly, but who also grew through that hurt to truly be a strong and sassy woman, whom I admire—no, change that, someone I still care for very much."

"Dada, more."

"Okay." He lifted Evie onto his lap and set the guitar in front of them. He picked out a sad tune. Sounded familiar. She closed her eyes. Listened to the lament.

Lament! That was it. The tune he'd picked out on her guitar at her apartment. Then he began to sing, putting words to the music. Sorrowful words, apologetic words, praising words, the tone of the music changing with each verse. She'd never heard anything more beautiful.

Then he set the guitar on the grass between them. "That's my gift for you."

"The song?"

He nodded.

She splayed a hand over her heart and looked to the sky twinkling blue between the leaves, and whispered. "Thank you."

"I also have a question for you."

Evie fought to stand, and he released her to toddle around.

"Do you suppose there's any way the two of us can start over? I'm the nerdy guy trying to look cool, playing on the worship team. You're the shy, talented, beautiful woman teaching Sunday school beneath the trees." He shook his head.

And she giggled.

He reached over and took her hand, ran his thumb across her palm, giving her goosebumps. The good kind.

"From the moment I saw you, Trip, er, Steph."

"I like Trip." She always had. To think a man cared enough about her to give her a pet name no one else had, made it special.

He grinned, his head constantly moving to keep an eye on Evie. "So, Trip, I crushed on you big time, and then you said, 'yes' when I asked you out. You couldn't have made me happier." He kissed the back of her hand. "I'm sorry I let us down, and I can't promise it would never happen again, but I look for approval from my Savior now, and no one else."

"So, you want to go out with me even if I'm no longer that shy, insecure girl?" Now, she was toying with him. Oh, yeah, she was all for going out with him again, but he deserved her answer being a little drawn out.

"I think who you are right now is pretty amazing. I love the bold and sassy vibe you have going now, and the way you faced your fear, talking at church? I think that made me fall for you all over again, and I really want to see if we can make us work. Will you give us a chance?"

"Hmm. I don't know." She tapped a finger to her lips. "Now this is really important."

"Okay..."

"Just wondering if you're still a really good kisser."

He grinned. "Is that an invitation?"

"Anyone ever tell you, you talk too much?" She got up on

her knees, cradled his stubble-covered cheeks between her hands and brushed her lips lightly over his. She leaned back and glanced in his moony eyes. "Does that answer your question?"

His lopsided smile matched his eyes. "Yeah, it does." He grabbed Evie as she motored past. "But I think our next date shouldn't include a squirmy one-year-old." He zerberted her stomach bringing a rush of giggles from all of them.

"Nope. She's a huge part of what made you who you are today, and I'm really liking you, so I suggest we keep her around."

"Hmm. I'm really liking you as well. Do you suppose we should kiss on it, seal our deal?" He leaned toward her, and Evie wriggled off his lap.

"Guess she doesn't want to come between us."

"Trip, I'm praying nothing will come between us again." And he kissed her soundly, definitely sealing the deal.

"Do not let any unwholesome talk come out of your mouths,
but only what is helpful for
building others up according to their needs,
that it may benefit those who listen."

– Ephesians 4:29 –

Dear Reader,

Social media is an amazing tool that can be used for so much good, but like anything else, when it's abused, it can cause great harm. Too often people forget to filter their words in the name of free speech. But just because something is legal doesn't make it right. I'm reminded of 1 Corinthians 10:23:

"All things are lawful," but not all things are helpful. "All things are lawful," but not all things build up.

As Stephenie Winter learned, it's always best to listen and learn before reacting. A good lesson for all of us, myself included.

You'll find further inspiration and encouragement on The Potter's House Books Website, (www.pottershousebooks.com) and by reading the other books in the series. Read them all and be encouraged and uplifted!

In Him,

Brenda

Find all the Potter's House books at

www.PottersHouseBooks.com.

Other Potter's House Books
By Brenda S. Anderson

HANDS OF GRACE
LONG WAY HOME
PLACE CALLED HOME
HOME ANOTHER WAY

Acknowledgements

Thank you to the seven other Potter's House Books (Two) authors who are sharing beautiful stories of God molding people's lives. It's a privilege writing alongside all of you!

Thanks also goes to:

My Book Booster Team ~ for tirelessly spreading the word about my books!

Glenn Winch ~ for your insider information on the life of a worship leader.

Lesley Ann McDaniel ~ for making my stories shine.

Gayle Balster ~ as always, for reading an early draft and offering encouragement.

Sarah, Bryan, and Brandon ~ for teaching me the ins and outs of social media!

My husband, Marvin ~ for enduring my disappearing act into my office these past several months and for always being my number one cheerleader.

And thank you, Jesus, for giving us wisdom to do what's right and for offering mercy for all those times we mess up.

About The Mosaic Collection

We are sisters, a beautiful mosaic united by the love of God through the blood of Christ.

An international group of authors releasing one book each month as we explore our theme, Family by His Design, and share stories that feature diverse, God-designed families. All are contemporary stories ranging from mystery to women's fiction, humorous fiction, and literary fiction. We hope you'll join our Mosaic family as we learn together what truly defines a family.

To keep informed about The Mosaic Collection books, subscribe to Grace & Glory, the official newsletter of The Mosaic Collection. You will receive monthly encouragement from Mosaic authors as well as timely updates about events, new releases, and giveaways.

Subscribe:
www.mosaiccollectionbooks.com/grace-glory/

Learn more about The Mosaic Collection at:
www.mosaiccollectionbooks.com/

Join our Reader Community, too!
www.facebook.com/groups/theMosaiccollection

COMING HOME SERIES

Praise for the Coming Home Series

"Anderson tackles family dynamics, tough issues, and gritty realism in her Coming Home series. From special needs babies to abortion and homelessness, you'll root for her authentic characters as they face real life struggles."

— Award-winning author, **Shannon Taylor Vannatter**

" . . . heartfelt, heart-wrenching fiction at its best, exploring relationships and family, love, faith and forgiveness in fresh, life-changing ways. I see myself in these endearing, enduring characters, their weaknesses and struggles and hard-won triumphs."

— **Laura Frantz**, author of *An Uncommon Woman*

"Anderson thrusts her readers into the gritty underbelly of family life and she doesn't mince words or shy away from the difficulties that complicate relationships. The reoccurring themes of grace and restitution are delivered with heart-wrenching honesty. These compelling stories celebrate the joys and sorrows of ordinary living with an extraordinary God."

— **Kav Rees**, BestReads-kav.blogspot.com

About the Author

Brenda S. Anderson writes gritty and authentic, life-affirming fiction. She is a member of the American Christian Fiction Writers, and is Past-President of the ACFW Minnesota chapter, MN-NICE, the 2016 ACFW Chapter of the Year. When not reading or writing, she enjoys music, theater, roller coasters, and baseball, and she loves watching movies with her family. She resides in the Minneapolis, Minnesota area with her husband of 30-plus years and one sassy cat.

Let's Connect

Visit Brenda online at www.BrendaAndersonBooks.com and on Facebook, Goodreads, Instagram, and BookBub.

For news and encouragement about upcoming books, contests, giveaways, and other activities, sign up for Brenda's bi-monthly newsletter.

If you enjoyed *Song of Mercy*, please consider leaving a review. Your words bring hope and encouragement to the author, as well as other readers.